residual
d e s i r e

residual
desire

J. Jill Robinson

COTEAU BOOKS
WWW.COTEAUBOOKS.COM

Edited by Edna Alford.
Book and cover design by Duncan Campbell.
Cover image, " Nude Woman/Sheet," by Jonathon Knowles /MASTERFILE.

Printed and bound in Canada at Gauvin Press.

National Library of Canada Cataloguing in Publication Data

Robinson, J. Jill, 1955-
Residual desire / J. Jill Robinson.

ISBN 1-55050-265-4

I. Title.
PS8585.O35166R47 2003   C813'.54   C2003-911243-8

1   2   3   4   5   6   7   8   9   10

401-2206 Dewdney Ave.
Regina, Saskatchewan
Canada   S4R 1H3

Available in the US and Canada from:
Fitzhenry & Whiteside
195 Allstate Parkway
Markham, Ontario
Canada   L3R 4T8

The publisher gratefully acknowledges the financial assistance of the Saskatchewan Arts Board, the Canada Council for the Arts, the Government of Canada through the Book Publishing Industry Development Program (BPIDP), and the City of Regina Arts Commission, for its publishing program.

For Steven and Emmett

contents

you *are* not *yourself* right *now*

*a*s I sit on the bus depot bench waiting for my father, I picture his grey hair, and the stoop in his shoulders from the crushed vertebrae that have begun to give him pain. I think about his blue eyes in his old man's face, and how the bones of his jaw and his skull become more and more apparent as he ages. How ingenuous the look in those blue eyes can be. My father is an old man: he is eighty-one. And his eyes seem to me to have become bluer. Is this possible?

Dad sails into the taxi zone in front of the bus depot in his big grey Chrysler. A taxi pulls in behind him and honks; the taxi driver waves his arms to motion the old man out of the zone. Very good, my good man. Very good there, says my father, waving back as he climbs out of his car. The taxi honks again, and my father pats the hood as he crosses in front of it and enters the depot through the wide open doors.

Dad takes me by the shoulders and murmurs in my ear, It's so good to see you, dear.

I think how it's like he's offering words of condolence at a funeral, or offering instructions on where to sit in a church. Gentleman that he is, decorum has always been my father's strong suit. Always gracious and polite. Well-mannered and proper. I slip my hands around him and give him a big hug.

Lovely to see you, he says.

Lovely to see *you,* I respond.

We drive home in an almost shy silence, broken only once when we are precisely halfway there. We see each other only once or twice a year, and it always takes us a little while to re-establish our rapport. Neither of us is uncomfortable with this: we have become accustomed.

Almost home! Dad says.

Sure are! I say gaily. And I smile to myself, because he always says exactly this, and he always says it right here, in front of Mr. Delancy's house. And next? Next, he will comment on the noisy little dog that lives there. Brownie.

That little dog who lives there – in that house right there – Dad says, pointing his arm across my face – he thinks it is funny to do this – is the most unpleasant little dog I've ever met! His name is Brownie, he adds with a hint of contempt. What a fascinating name, don't you think? Brownie.

Does he bite?

He'd take a nip out of you in an instant.

Good thing he's behind the fence, I say, stealing his next line.

Well, yes! Dad says, surprised. That's right! That's just what I was thinking.

And then we are silent, but companionable, until he pulls into the driveway. The first thing I notice is how overgrown the yard is — it could use some serious attention with the clippers. Or the scythe. The ferns on either side of the driveway are gigantic; the weeds, everywhere, are three feet high, overwhelming the legitimate plants.

The bead Dad has hung to indicate when the car is all the way into the carport plunks against the windshield, and Dad jerks on the brakes.

Here we go! he says, and slaps my bare leg lightly. Out you get!

The rhododendrons are huge, too. The red one outside the front door is about to burst into bloom. It has grown at least a foot since last year — it easily reaches up to my bedroom window now. The plants around here are certainly thriving, anyway, I think. Getting better with age. That's something.

Once we are inside, Dad says, Well, dear, can I get you a drink?

Sure, I say. Do you have any Diet Coke?

Why, yes! he says. I believe I have some of that. Never drink it myself, but when company comes.... He points to the fridge.

On the floor beside the fridge stand three or four two-litre bottles of pop, some empty, some partly full. The Diet Coke looks suspiciously like the one I bought at Christmas – it has the same sale sticker. I unscrew the lid and no sound escapes.

This pop is dead, I say.

Dead! It can't be! Are you sure?

Positive. I put my hand over the end and give the bottle a shake. Nothing. Completely, I say. I think this is the pop I bought at Christmas.

Well get something else, then. But I'm sure it's perfectly fine.

Not if it's six months old, I say, turning away. The telephone rings as I move over to the sink. Dad answers it as I start to pour the dark liquid down the drain.

No, I don't think so, he says into the receiver. The house was painted last year.

Then he glances over and sees what I am doing. He wildly gesticulates, and hangs up the phone with a bang and rushes over to the sink. He wrenches the bottle from my hands.

What are you doing?! What do you think you're doing?!

The pop's no good, Dad, I say, startled, defensive. That's all. I'm throwing it out.

It's my pop!

I know Dad, but –

I would have drunk it.

Dad.

I like it flat. I'm not fussy like you.

Dad.

It was mine. You had no right to do that. No right at all.

I'm sorry.

4

Angrily, he screws the lid back on the bottle. Shaking his head, sighing deeply, he shoots me an injured look and replaces the bottle beside the others. He holds up a half-empty bottle of Sprite.

There's this, he says. You could try this if you want to.

No thanks, I say. I'll make some tea.

I had intended to cook supper for him. I wanted it to be like old times, the two of us together. I would present my culinary creation, he would offer a critique. Then we would do the dishes together. I thought we could go grocery shopping together, too, something new, and I had composed a shopping list while I sat on the bus.

I guess we should start thinking about supper, I say as an introduction. I open the fridge door to see what he has on hand, but before I can look inside he shuts it again. Wait a minute, he says. You just wait there one minute.

I was just going to look in the fridge, Dad.

Never mind that, he says. I have these coupons. Look!

He gets a seniors discount at a Chinese takeout just up the hill beside the gas station, and he has been waiting for the opportunity to use it. The menu contains the standard Canadian pseudo-Chinese food: we order mushroom egg foo yung; beef chow mein; egg rolls; chicken fried rice. I find some chopsticks in the back of the silverware drawer. Dad goes into his bedroom and emerges with a bottle of white wine.

It isn't Chinese wine, he says, but I guess it will do!

Some sort of equilibrium has been reached, I think, relaxing a little. Dad is pleasant and calm as he helps set the table. I pass him bowls and water glasses. The soya sauce, napkins, and serving spoons. He gets two wine glasses from the china cabinet. We clink our glasses together in a mutual toast. The delivery man brings the food. I pay and tip him.

As we munch egg rolls, Dad says, What is this sauce, do you suppose?

I look at him in surprise. Just soya sauce.

Soya sauce? I've never heard of such a thing. It's very nice for dipping.

Sure you have, Dad. Soya sauce.

I know what I've had and what I haven't, he says quietly.

Yes, I say. Of course you do.

Dad follows the wine with two rye and waters. Then he looks over at me sadly. I am eighty-one years old, he says. Can you believe it?

I guess I'll have to, Dad, I say gently.

I can hardly believe it myself. I look at myself in the mirror, and I say, *I am more than eighty years old!* It has to be so: there I am! But it is hard to believe.

Does it bother you?

It bothers me that I can't do all the things I used to do.

I know.

You know? You know? What do you know about it? He rises meaningfully, puts his serviette down on his bread-and-butter plate, takes his glass over to the sideboard and pours himself another drink.

I get up to clear the table. He follows me into the

kitchen. What do you know? he says. He pokes me in the shoulder. What do you know about anything?

Nothing, I say. My fist is full of chopsticks. I feel like I'm ten.

Nothing is right! He pokes me again. That's *exactly* right! *Nothing*.

Dad, *stop* it.

He stops. Then he pauses, and says, Well. Just so you know. And he returns to the living room. He sits down in his favourite chair – I bought it for him when he retired – and picks up the weekend crossword. He is like an island, I think, rubbing my shoulder. That space in the living room is his Cuba. The standing lamp behind him lights the page. His drink sits on a small table beside him, and beside the drink is the remote, and the cordless phone. Beyond the TV is the picture window which allows him to see people come up the driveway. Through the space between the curtains.

I'll sleep in the room which used to be mine but is now the general guest room. There are pictures on the wall and on top of the dresser, of me at various ages, and of Dad when he was a child, and then a young man. There's no point looking for space to put my things. I know that all the dresser drawers are full, and so is the closet. There's Christmas wrapping in one drawer, sewing supplies in another, and in the third a mix: a pair of boxer shorts with a seam gone; a set of old photos with an elastic band around them; a jar of buttons which has spilled; a bumper sticker about loving country music, and some coupons. In the closet and under the bed are plastic shopping bags and clothing that is ripped, missing buttons, or too small. I leave my clothes in my suitcase, take out my cosmetic bag and make room for it on top of the dresser by shoving the piles of paperback mysteries to one end, then stacking them higher.

When I come out of my room to say goodnight, Dad is still sitting in his favourite chair. I kiss the top of his head, and his cheek.

Sleep well, dear, he says, and pats my hand.

You too, Dad. I'm very glad to see you, you know.

I'm glad to see you, too, dear.

I read a while – Grace Paley – but find it difficult to concentrate. The TV blares from the living room. But I'm not going to ask him to turn it down. It is his house, and if he wants the TV on like that, fine. I wake up at around three to the sound of the television's off-air signal. I slip out of bed. My father is still in his chair, the remote clutched in his hand. I worry as I walk towards him, as I always do now, that he has died, and that when I touch him he will be cold. But he isn't. I take the control from his hands and turn off the TV. Dad, I whisper loudly. Dad, wake up. It's time to go to bed.

What? What's that? I was watching that! he says.

Dad, it's time for bed. It's three o'clock in the morning.

Oh, all right, he says sleepily. I offer him my arm. Here, Dad.

I don't need that, he says, slapping my hand away. I can manage just fine.

Is my father more himself now, or less? I wonder, as I try to get back to sleep. This rudeness, these unkindnesses, have they always been there, but well covered by deeply conditioned social grace? My father, the gentleman. Does the veneer of civilized behaviour wear through when you age? What is making him like this? Who is he turning into?

One of the stories my father used to tell me is about how peculiar his grandfather became late in life. Your uncle and I would go to Calgary for our piano lessons every week, Dad would say, and we would visit our grandparents while we were there, and often we played the piano. But Grandfather was becoming more fervent in his religion as he aged, and he decided that he didn't want us playing jazz. So Grandmother took us aside and asked us to stick to classical pieces from then on, so we wouldn't upset him. A while later, she said that he didn't want us playing classical music either: only hymns.

Eventually they were to play nothing at all, for it made the old man suspicious beyond endurance. He was becoming more and more deaf, and couldn't be sure they were playing only hymns. And when he was suspicious, he got agitated, explained their grandmother, and agitation was bad for his heart. So the two boys sat and looked out the window. There was nothing to do at their grandparents' house, if they couldn't play the piano. No cards, either, of course. Everything was suspect. Everything might contain a drop of the devil. Except the Bible, and who wanted to read that? Some of these old guys, Dad said each time he told the story, get funny in the head. You have to expect it. The body and mind deteriorate. It's a natural process.

I can't sleep, so I get up and wander into the kitchen. I open the fridge door. I bask in the cool air with my eyes closed, until the fridge's motor kicks in. Then I look inside. It's one hell of a mess. In one freezer dish is a furry, grey mound. In another is something that has turned into green liquid – perhaps a green pepper. Cheese in a variety of colours, none of them yellow or orange. Rust-coloured dust seeps out of a cardboard box of raisins in a side shelf. I close the door.

At six-thirty, the CBC comes on in a giant blast, and I lie in bed listening to a discussion about the cost of calves and pigs, and the price of last year's wheat and canola. My father never farmed, but the idea has appealed to him in the last couple of years, as he reminisces more. Your grandfather, he has told me, worked his way across Canada the summer he started law school. He stopped in Saskatchewan and got a job stooking wheat. It was hard work, but satisfying, and he seriously considered staying with the farming and foregoing Queen's. Ready money was very tempting. But his affianced, your grandmother, wouldn't hear of it. She wanted to be married to a professional man, not a farmer. But if he hadn't listened to her, if he had stayed longer in Saskatchewan, or Manitoba, you might be sitting in a farm kitchen now, instead of here.

Thank you, Grandma, I say, stretching in bed.

At six-fifty Dad knocks on my door and says, Are you getting up?

In a minute, Dad, I say. I want to lie in bed a couple of minutes longer, listen to the birds waking up outside my window, watch the blue sky lighten.

Dad planted that big red rhodo outside the window years ago, when he and I had just moved into this subdivision from our leafy acreage, had left the stream and woods and place I was born. My mother had left the year before, had left the cherry and holly trees and us without a second's regard or regret. We were glad she was gone, I told my friends. Both Dad and I were glad. Then we moved to this brand new, white subdivision house. I made his meals. I did the ironing. I kept an eye on the cleaning woman. I was sixteen then.

The house has never been painted in those twenty-five years – no matter what Dad tells people – and it's a grubby white inside and out. The forest green trim on the outside has faded and worn down to the original wood. The wooden eavestroughs are full and rotting. Inside the house, the original base coat on the scarred walls is chipped and stained. The two-tone red and orange shag carpet in the living room, dining room, and hall has never been cleaned, lies flattened in paths. No amount of encouragement from the vacuum cleaner will make it rise. The long, flowered curtains, new when the house was new, have never been cleaned, have never in fact been opened or closed since we first moved here, as far as I know, because the pulleys don't work. And so the curtains remain fixed, open three feet. Gathering dust. Stopped.

Dad knocks again on my door. Go away, I whisper through my teeth. Go away, Dad.

Are you getting up, dear? The coffee is ready. I've got the cereal out. I'll be having a banana on my cereal. Would you like one? There's just the one more.

I don't know. I'll be out in a minute, Dad.

I am famous for being grouchy in the morning. For needing two cups of coffee before I talk to anyone. He must not remember. I go into the kitchen, silently take out a mug and fill it with coffee. My father has his back to me. The paper is propped up in front of him. I can hear the crunch of his cereal as he eats. Quietly I pour cream into the coffee, then pick up my mug and try to sneak out of the kitchen.

Where are you going?

Dad, I'll be out in a few minutes. You know how I am in the morning.

He twists his head around and peers at me.

No, I don't know how you are in the morning. What do you mean?

I just need a few minutes to myself. To wake up.

You need to eat a decent breakfast is what you need to do.

I will have a good breakfast, Dad.

Can't go without fuel. Your body needs fuel. He slides his chair out, gets up, comes towards me. Break the fast, that's what you need to do. Break the fast. Here. Here's your cereal. Now he is standing up in front of me, pressing a cereal bowl into my chest.

I see red. I want to grab the bowl from his hands and pitch it across the room.

Dad I *know*, I say, stepping back. I *will*. I don't *want* that, Dad. I *know* about breakfast. I am going on forty-two. You taught me. But I am going to have a few minutes.

He shakes his head angrily, turns his back.

I shut my bedroom door firmly. Hear the newspaper

snap. My heart is pounding with anger. I am shaking. Watch out, I say to myself. Watch out. You are not yourself right now.

In a few minutes I hear him rise, then come to stand outside my door. I sit still and silent, freeze as though I am in a game of statues. Then he knocks.

You're not smoking in there, are you?

No. I don't smoke.

I can smell something.

No, you can't.

He opens the door. If you quit smoking, that would be welcome news, he says firmly.

I don't smoke. I have never smoked.

His expression immediately changes. In less than a second he goes from confident and fatherly to uncertain and confused. Oh, Dad. I sigh a big sigh. Wish I hadn't corrected him. It wouldn't have killed me.

Are you ready for breakfast? he says. I've sliced your banana. It will go brown if it sits too long.

I'll be right out.

I think that's best, he says.

In the beautiful, sunny morning we walk together in a nature park near his house. We walk through cedars and fir, down a gully, along dirt paths that remind me of the home we left. The smells. The touch of leaves and branches. My father was seldom at home in those days. But when he was home, we were often outside together. I watched him build things, prune things, dig things, and sometimes he would teach me how. But he was frequently away from the house working, or feigning work.

There is no need for conversation in this communion, I think happily, and we walk along companionably, until my father trips on a root that sticks out of the dirt path, like a hard vein. He falls heavily against me, clutches my arm to break his fall. He is a big man, and I almost fall too.

Are you okay, Dad? I say, once we have righted ourselves and stand, somewhat shaken, on the side of the path. Do you want to sit down for a minute?

I'll be fine.

Are you sure?

Yes.

But he doesn't look fine. He seems sad, subdued, as we walk on, and he is clearly still unsteady. Then he says, You know, it bothers me that I can't trust my legs anymore. I used to have good balance. For walking, for hiking. But now I can't trust myself at all. I don't like that much.

Do you want to go back? Should we go back? We could. Right now. Or I could go and get the car.

I'm not a goner yet, he says. We're going to finish this walk.

After lunch at the Kentucky Fried Chicken on Bennett Highway, Dad drives me over to the bus depot. He parks in the loading zone, gets out of the car and carries my bag to the platform. Then I walk him back to his car. We have had a good visit, I think. Overall. Dad opens his arms to hug me goodbye. I move into them, put my head against his chest. I can hear his heart. I can smell his special smell. I love how his hands feel on my shoulders. As I do every time I visit now, I wonder if this will be the last time I hear his heart beating like this, the last time I feel the warmth of his skin against mine.

Goodbye, Dad, I say. I love you.

I love you too, dear, he says. And then he steps back, off the curb, and he loses his balance. He flails as he tries to grab onto me, but he falls. His head hits the car's bumper and then the ground. Jesus, I say. Dad. I crumple beside him. A cabby leaps out of his car and rushes over. I smell American cigarettes. Dad? Dad? I say. My father opens his eyes. In them is confusion, and hurt. Then his eyes fill with a sky blue blankness, and close again. I see blood seeping into his hair.

Several hours later I drive up Dad's driveway alone. The bead hits the windshield. Plunk. I heave myself out of Dad's car and walk slowly into his house and up his stairs. I wander down the hall and into his room, and lie on his bed. I can smell him. God, I feel tired. Completely wiped out, and strange. How close I came to his death.

The gash in his skull required five stitches; it must have been like sewing tissue paper for whoever put them in. Dad will be in the hospital for a day or two, for observation, and then I can bring him home. He hates being anywhere but home. I don't want to remember the desperate look in those blue eyes as I left him.

Where are you going? he whispered. Where are you going, dear? I had to pry his fingers to make him let go of my arm, and it took all my strength. Now I am so tired I can barely move. I drag the quilt up around me, and over my head.

Later I return to the kitchen, open the fridge door and stand in the cold air. It feels good after the warmth of the bed. Growth and decay, I think, as my eyes fall again on the raisin dust, on the liquefied green pepper, on the cheese. What an odd mixture. Nothing in its original form.

déjà *vu*

*e*d didn't want to stop in Calgary. He wanted to get out to the convention at the coast, dammit. But Iris managed to talk him into stopping – just overnight, Ed, she said. You can get a little R & R while I do some shopping. All right, honey? I need some things for the trip.

Just don't take all day, okay? grumbled Ed. That's all I ask.

She got him a copy of the *Real Estate Weekly* and left him talking condos on his cellphone in a coffee shop near the motel. Iris got behind the wheel of the Eldorado and drove over to her old house, to visit Larry. Go through these lights, turn here, turn here. The moves came back to her readily, and she travelled to the house and into the driveway, parked and got out as smoothly and easily as a silk scarf would slip over her arm.

She was surprised her heart started to pump wildly in the driveway, started to ache as she approached the front door. She hadn't thought she'd feel anything other than a mild interest. She thought she and her ex-husband would have a nice little chat. Get caught up. That it would be fun, a lark even, to see Larry again for a few minutes – no big deal. But she couldn't say a thing when Larry came to the door in answer to her knock, because she was about to burst into tears. Her heart was like an off-kilter washing machine. She waved her hand in a foolish, mute greeting. Gasped for deep breath and walked right past Larry and his warm, surprised smile. Hi there, he said as she entered the house. Welcome home.

Iris didn't go any further than the foyer before she stopped dead. The pictures on the walls were right where she had hung them when she and Larry moved in. The ceramic dish was still where she had placed it on the sideboard; the ashtray was still in the centre of the dining-room table. Hadn't moved an inch. The green quilted hassock he liked to sit on when he took off his workboots. The mustard yellow recliner they bought at a garage sale one Saturday afternoon. The maple dining-room suite from his parents. The oil painting from her parents. And him, Larry, her ex-husband, standing there with love – is that what it was? – in his eyes. She'd forgotten about him, as well, forgotten how he could make her feel. Like the other things that had taken up space in what she had come to call her old life, much of him had become vague, grey, and fuzzy.

You know how you think you'll always remember something? How when some romantic exchange, some terrible small act of violence, some gorgeous view, has a big impact on you, and you go to save it carefully in your memory bank, or take a picture, you tell yourself, Don't bother. Don't waste the film. You won't ever forget this. But you do. Then you are astounded at yourself when you realize that you *have* forgotten it. Again. That you have never learned and will never never learn this simple fact: people forget. That's the way it is.

The quality and degree of emotion in Larry's eyes filled their lovely greenness completely. When she still lived here, there was always love for her in those eyes, she remembered now in a rush, even when he was furious at something she had said or done. Bewilderment, pain, exasperation – there had been those. Plenty, plenty of those. But there was always love as well.

They had lived together in this house for only six months. Buying it was part of the final hare-brained scheme she had conjured up to save them. Maybe this is what we need, she had said. Maybe we just need more room.

A bigger mortgage, he had responded gloomily. That'll give us room. Sure. No point in arguing with you, he added, pouring himself a scotch, when you've got one of your ideas.

May I borrow your bathroom, Larry? Iris said in a tear-choked whisper.

Sure, said Larry. Just don't forget to give it back.

Iris sat on the toilet with her head in her hands and her eyes closed. She took deep, long breaths until she could stop crying and her jumbled mind was blank again, until her hands could sit still in her lap.

Then she blew her nose and washed her hands with a cake of dirty soap. Dried them on a lilac-coloured towel from a set she and Larry had bought on a shopping trip to the States. She opened the drawer that used to be hers. In it was a package of razor blades, a travel pack of Kleenex, and Larry's wedding ring, loose. She picked up the ring. Slipped it onto her finger. It was twice as big as hers had been. His hands weren't big, but his fingers were. She took the ring off again. Kissed it, then held it in her fist for a few seconds before she replaced it in the drawer. I miss you, Larry, she said.

To put her wedding ring on again and go back into her old life would be so nice right now. To leave the tight, hard, clenched life she now led. Her old life was right here, so familiar, as familiar and safe as an old coat, its worn mauve fabric against her cheek. How appealing that was. Collar up, three or four large, round buttons, frayed cuffs, holes in the pockets.

She looked up, looked hard at herself in the big oval mirror. She looked sad.

Way back, when they started dating, which was also when they started fighting, she said one day, I wish we could sweep all the crap off this sidewalk, Larry. I wish we could get rid of the dead leaves, and the dropped milkshake, and the cigarette butts. She had remembered this conversation over the years because she liked that she had thought up the comparison herself and that it was so apt. Larry just nodded unhappily when she said it. He hated fighting, and so much of what they did was fight. She, however, had always thought it was normal. Her family fought all the time. Not fisticuffs, but words. Ambushes and grenades. Word bombs and bayonets. She tried to explain this to Larry, explain that it was healthy to express your feelings like that. I don't think so, he said numbly. It isn't natural for me. I feel like I've been beat up, he said. Oh Larry, she said. You have to get tougher.

Oftentimes she couldn't remember what she had been mad about any more than she could remember what she had had for lunch. Being mad was simply a part of her, like breathing. Anger came and went, came and went. Like joy. But no one had ever yelled at him before, Larry said. Not your Mum? she had asked. No, he said. Never.

I can't remember my mother *not* yelling, Iris said.

Larry endured, and survived, and found some armour – the liquid kind – and they kept on going. But instead of a swept sidewalk, there was further accumulation. Over the years refuse grew so thick that eventually they couldn't see the sidewalk, gave up believing that there ever had been a path for them. If she mentioned the possibility of change, or her search for hope, Larry, sitting with his drink in that mustard yellow recliner, just said Hmm? Hmm? Or ignored her.

You should change, she used to tell him.

Two things, she said, standing in front of the TV screen so he couldn't see anything but her. First, you should not allow me to be this way. I'm mean to you. I say things I shouldn't. I walk all over you and I bitch all the time. You should demand that I mend my ways or else.

That's *your* problem, Larry said, yawning. Not mine. Would you move, please?

Secondly, she said, ignoring his request, you should change. You shouldn't sit there in front of the TV like that. You used to be much more interesting. My advice to you is don't give me anything to complain about, and that will make a big difference.

Right, he said. Move out of the way, would you?

I'll leave, she began to threaten. I can't live here like this.

Don't leave, he said, and at first he meant it. I love you. Don't go.

Then she met Ed, and to her own surprise her threat was no longer idle.

Ed the Great. Ed who was everything on any list she'd ever made. Snazzy dresser. Free with the cash. Funny. Sexy as all hell and hot to trot. And, best of all, she was never angry anymore. All that guilt could stop accumulating. Not that he would have put up with her being mad anyway. He wouldn't have. I'm here for a good time, not a long time, Juanita, he said. Keep that in mind.

Ed liked to call her Juanita. She called him Pedro. Her body thrilled whenever he appeared, and she thought she had been reborn. He was like all those songs. He swept her up. Swept her away. Swept her out of the new driveway in his Eldorado.

Larry, I'm really leaving, she said.

If that's what you have to do, he said.

Don't you care?

Of course I care. Do you care, Iris?

My feelings are complex, she said.

You never spoke a truer word, said Larry. I agree with you a hundred percent on that one.

The day before she left, they walked on the bluff behind their place. Walked the trails they always walked, watched their neighbour's dog take off after gophers and birds. She said to Larry, You said once that if I left you would ask me to stay. But now, when I'm going for sure, you haven't asked me to stay. You haven't said don't go. You haven't done a thing.

It's too late for that, he said to her. We're too far gone for that.

And now? Now she is in the dustbin. What an idiot she has been.

She is *not* everything-that-was-ever-on-his-list to Ed. And Ed doesn't do flowers, or cards, or phone calls when he's going to be late, the way Larry used to. And if she gets mad, he tells her to leave. Ship out, Iris, Ed says. Or cut the crap.

And, to be honest, it was not *if* she got mad, it was *when*. And that was more and more often. The anger had only fooled her into thinking it was gone.

Lately when Ed looks at her, there is no love in his eyes; in fact, there have been flashes of what resembles dislike.

Maybe you should think of going back there, he said one day, a new nastiness in his voice. Maybe you are in the wrong place.

Maybe I am.

That's probably where you should be. Back there in Cowtown with Larry.

Ed, do you really think that's where I should be?

Give it a rest, would you? Just lighten up, and things will be all right. Okay?

But she can't lighten up. This is her life, and she's the only one who can watch out for her, the only one who really cares what happens to her. When she and Ed fool around, she feels farther away instead of closer when it's over and he's pulling on his pants. And worse, she feels she could have been anyone. Is it *her* making herself feel this way? Or him? She can't tell.

What have I done? she has asked herself in the middle of some nights. What, oh what, have I done?

You made your bed, she has answered herself in her mother's voice. Now lie in it.

Larry, oh, Larry. Larry who used to bring her lilacs. One year when she came back from a trip he picked her up at the airport with his van full of them. The smell was to die for.

Eight and a half years she was married to him. Husband and wife. Need a shelf above the stove? Need a hole dug in the garden? Need to be held, feel safe, feel warm? Larry would always oblige.

You're my #1, he'd tell her, and she'd roll her eyes. He

bought her big sucky and gushy cards for her birthday and Christmas. "My Better Half." A part of her had sneered. He sent her gargantuan flower arrangements on their anniversaries. She thought him sentimental, and a fool.

Iris left the bathroom. Larry was making coffee; she could smell it, and she headed for the kitchen. While the coffee brewed he would give her a tour of the house, he said. He pointed out the changes he had made since she had left, and she admired those changes, starting with the new lino in the kitchen.

But *I* wouldn't have chosen that colour, Lar, Iris said.

With laughter in his eyes Larry said, That's why I chose it, Iris. I've finally got a mind of my own.

He showed her how he had installed a bevelled glass window in a space by his office. How he had refinished the hardwood in what had been her sewing room and was now a guest bedroom. And then they went outside and he showed her how he had added fake grass carpet to the deck, and he showed her the new downspouts on each corner of the house, each of them pointing away.

Very nice, she said lightly. You have my full approval, Lar.

Then, right there on the lawn, Larry turned to her and took her in his arms. He hugged her close and took her breath away. He said, Iris. Iris.

She could stay there forever, she thought, it felt so good. She started to shake. She was being given a choice. She knew it. There was magic at work. She had come on the right day, when the right magic was in the air, the right music was playing. She could stay, resume her old life. She could walk into the house and into the kitchen, open the fridge and recognize everything in it. She could go to the front closet and slip on the cardigan she liked to wear when she was puttering around the house. She could. She really and truly could.

Ed? Ed was far, far away. She could barely see him in her mind – he was a teeny tiny figure at a little wee table in a distant Robin's Donuts. With his head still buried in the *Real Estate Weekly.*

When she had first found out about Ed's affair, she'd thought about Larry, and wished he were there to comfort her, to take her in his arms like this. She lay on the bed crying, and imagined Larry as he hugged her, saying, Iris, Iris, Oh Honey, Oh Dear. She thought that she would give anything to be in his arms. Hearing those familiar words. How nice it was that Larry never changed. Larry could be counted on.

Ed, she said now. And stopped.

Ed what? Larry pulled away from her.

He loves someone else, she wanted to say. And it hurts so much.

Ed nothing, she said. Ed nothing.

And there was a short, uncomfortable silence, into which all possibility vanished. Larry and Iris stared at the downspouts.

It was nice to see you, Larry said finally, and turned toward the Eldorado. Come again. Anytime.

Sure Lar, Iris said lightly. Thanks. She took three steps and turned back to him. And said, with tears in her eyes, Larry, I'm so sorry for all that went wrong between us.

There was a pause, and then Larry said, So am I.

But it was always wrong, wasn't it Lar? she said, pleading. We weren't the right people for each other. We always fought. Always. Didn't we?

Iris, nobody's perfect, said Larry. Nobody. Not even you, though you were pretty darn close in my book. Remember that.

There was a toothpick hanging out of Ed's mouth as he drove, and he made it bob up and down with his tongue as he whistled through his teeth. He glanced over at her.

You getting a cold? he asked.

Yes, she said.

Here's some Kleenex, he said, and threw over a box.

Thank you, she said, and turned her head away.

Larry had gone through a hailstorm for her once, ran down the sidewalk in the backyard of their first little house through pelting hailstones, ran toward the garage to get his painting sheets to drape over her tomato plants. He came out of the garage laden with sheets and with his yellow hard hat on. He stopped, looked up, waved at her with a big smile. That was Larry all over. No pizzazz, no electricity. Just good-natured, good-hearted loving.

And she didn't want it. Couldn't want it.

And that was still the case.

Love didn't always conquer all, not by a long shot. And no amount of magic could truly have cleansed the angry, resentful, hurtful old life she had made them lead, the one with hostility plastered thick and hard on every surface. Not a chance. Not a hope. She deserved anything that happened to her. And she had better be willing to face the music.

So, Ed, she said, tossing her Kleenex towards the garbage bag. Tell me about this Juanita.

walking *on* air

*O*ut in the mushroom barn, or mending a fence over at the doctor's next door, in any split second Andy could see in his mind's eye Leah's pale red hair, pale freckled hands, faded green coat; her peaked brown scarf, her gumboots, and always, always, the fear in her darting brown eyes. She and Andy haven't been able to rid themselves of that. In these moments of picturing her, Andy could always feel the thick blend of his love and concern as it rose and travelled, heavy and sluggish, as though through his bowels.

Leah's fear.

It was true. No denying it. There *had* been many deaths in the neighbourhood; that in itself was peculiar. Most people would use words like coincidence or odd and be done with it, but it was something else, some-thing more, to Leah. To her, the neighbourhood was under a spell. Not the work of the Christian devil, it was more a moody cloak of evil, though she did call it male, a giant, present force of Evil that scared her witless and made her watch for signs of its reappearance every minute of the day and night, made her look for him – though she had never actually seen him, couldn't actually describe him – in the unlikeliest of places.

He made fog, she would repeat to Andy as she gave again the litany of deaths, and Mrs. Caldwell drove into the river. He gave him the rope, and Billy Adamson hanged himself. He gave her pills, and Lois Brown slept to death. He crushed the boy, Andrew Simchuk, as he fixed his car. He burned the box factory down, with Jim the watchman inside.

Can't you *see?* she said earnestly, white hands clenching each other in a tight, knuckle-hard ball. Andy, you must *see* that we are next? Our house, and the doctor's. The doctor and Mrs. Doctor. Their little girls. We're the only ones left!

The doctor's tall, imposing house stands next door to Andy and Leah's matchbox stucco, with a copse of trees and a fence in between. Huge glass windows overlook the doctor's front lawn and the grape and rose arbours, and it's a long walk from the front door around the body of the house to the back where Andy is supposed to knock when he works for them.

Mrs. Doctor, short and buxom, waters her hanging baskets by the gate between the properties, waters with a long-handled, long-spouted watering can, little bunches of oil-paint violets on either side. Mrs. Doctor, in her camel hair coat and her black leather driving gloves, leaves *Vogue* and *McCall's* magazines for Leah in the basket at the gate.

Andy sees the doctor's black lab with one of Andy's chickens around its neck. Rotting, stinking corpse of a chicken. That woman is a cruel one, he thinks. Took off her leather driving gloves and tied that chicken on two weeks ago. Don't Touch Those Chickens, Bad Dog.

Look at the goddam sadness and shame on that dog's face, Andy said to Leah. In that dog's eyes. Being punished for going after them. There must be another way.

She'd put that look into her four daughters if she could, said Leah.

In the front room one Sunday morning, tucked under the sewing machine like a gift under the tree at Christmas, was a little girl. Smiling up at Leah and asking to push the treadle.

I've come to visit before Sunday school, she said, waving tiny white-gloved hands. Am I too early?

Never, my sweet, said Leah. Leah, whom Andy found weeping in the kitchen as she put on the kettle. Leah, all gentleness, who longs for a child. Not a drop of meanness in her, while the little girls' mother boils their breakfasts in it.

Another of the little girls is learning to read; she sits on the clothesline platform and reads out loud to Leah in a small clear voice as Leah hangs out the clothes: "When the autumn comes, the leaves will fall. When the winter comes, there will be snow."

Let me! Please let me! Leah cried when Andy found her in the kitchen, covers off the wood stove, fire licking the ceiling, the wall behind the stove black, smoking, stinking. Him jumping out of his skin and grabbing for towels to wet, and clanging to get those covers back in place and keep the house from burning down to the ground. Holy Jesus! Holding her by the wrists. Leah, Leah.

Before he does! she cried, wrestling, pulling. Let me burn it up before he does! Her face hot, sweaty with fear.

Burned *up,* she said afterwards, holding out her teacup to him. Up, Andy. Not *down.* I'd never burn it *down.*

He was washing up and she was standing in the doorway.

I would have left you nowheres to live, Andy, she said sadly, putting the cup tenderly on the counter beside the sink, and touching its rim gently with one finger before she pulled her hand away. You would have had to live in the mushroom barn, or in the doctor's boat, Andy.

Did you take your pills, Leah? he asked.

I don't remember, she said.

Andy couldn't find her at first, though he looked everywhere he could think of. He found her only when he heard her speaking as she sat in the bedroom closet.

"He lurks in the trilliums under the trees," came her muffled voice.

"Daily Bread," she answered.

"He's in the twisted vine maples, above and below the earth," she said.

"Bless This House," she answered.

"He's in the deep of the stream."

"Yes," she answered. "He's behind the house, in the well, the shed. He's coming up our driveway. He's bringing my death like a kitten."

I don't want to, Leah whispered to Andy as he held out a glass of water and her pills.

They're good, Leah. They'll help you.

I don't want to, she whispered. Please.

Leah. Listen. You have to. Here.

At the gate, Mrs. Doctor stands screaming beneath the hanging baskets. Fuchsia and begonias sway above her hot, black anger. A cast-iron frying pan is flung on the ground. She cooks then, thinks Andy, ambling towards her; that woman actually stands in front of a stove! She takes mushrooms, she takes an egg Andy has sold her, cracks it, watches it slip into melted butter. She stands waving a spatula.

You! You see what's happened! Her voice is shrill. Andy! Get over here and see what has happened! Look! You! Andy!

A moment after Andy sees, the dog appears and gobbles up the partially formed chick, then licks the frying pan clean. Mrs. Doctor runs off, hysterical. Ten yards away she stops, turns, calls back to Andy. You won't sell us *anything* anymore, comes her hard, trembling voice. *Anything.* Do you hear? Andy takes the frying pan home, washes it with an SOS pad in the sink, oils it, takes it back later; sets the pan on the patio table when he's over there pruning blackberries.

Oh dear, says Leah when he tells her. Oh dear. Dear. Leah, you've got to be more careful about the eggs.

More careful? she says. All right.

Through his sleep Andy thinks he hears Leah say, Sleep tight, sleep safe. I will take care. She slips into the night with a kitchen knife, slips into the black, wet night without waking him.

Her brown woollen hat has long arms to wrap round her neck as a muffler. The hay is wet and high to walk through. Wet skirt, wet gumboots, bare feet inside. Once through the hayfield, she makes her way through bush over to the fence. She catches the skirt of her dress on the barbed wire as she climbs over, awkward because of the knife. She crouches down and takes her skirt in her hand; she talks to the rent as she strokes the fabric: Now there will be mending.

Andy gets up out of bed, goes to the doctor's house looking for her. Rain drips from his hat and his cloth coat as he rings the doorbell, which sounds like church chimes. The doctor himself comes, opens the door in his blue striped pyjamas and burgundy dressing gown.

Good God, man, it's three in the morning. Yes. She was here. But she's gone now. We could hear her outside the bedroom window. I couldn't make sense of what she said. She must take her pills. Do you understand? They will calm her down. *These people,* he whispers as he shuts the door.

On her birthday morning, Leah saw Andy's truck turn up the driveway. She watched the truck bounce through the road's hollows – he drove faster than usual, and the water splashed out of the puddles and washed the mud off the tires and hubcaps.

She walked into the yard to meet him, and when he got out of the truck she could tell there was something tucked inside the front of his overalls, but he was pretending otherwise, and so she did too.

Town was good, he said.

She nodded.

Happy Birthday, he said, and his body mewed. From the front of his overalls he drew a grey kitten, placed it gently in her hands. Leah bent her head over the mewing, ran her fingers softly against fur the colour of storm clouds. Mew.

Tootsie, said Leah.

Leah looked at Andy over the head of her kitten, followed his shifting feet and the legs of the blue denim overalls, looked up along his chest and then into his shyly pleased and hopeful face. Andy didn't always wear his teeth, and his mouth would sag, soft and pliant without them, like now. Like a sea anemone's mouth, if she put her finger in.

Thank you, she said.

Happy Birthday, he said.

They spent the afternoon at White Rock beach. Strands of green and brown seaweed washed slowly in the easy tide, and the gulls called, circled idly, called again. Fragments of grey sheets, of bleached white tea towels, spinning and swooping in the ocean's spring wind. It was a warm day at the beach, people digging, sitting on logs, walking along the beach or down the railway tracks above it, balancing.

In her faded yellow dress Leah stands calmly by a bank of blackberries, below the tracks, with the kitten in the crook of her arm or in her cotton knitting bag with the wooden handles, small head peeking out. Andy comes up beside her. He's taken his shoes off, and the sand has covered his feet. Underdone doughnuts rolled in grey sugar, she says and smiles. Happy? he asks. So happy I'm walking on air, she says. She laughs at his walking on stones, at his white-foot "ouches," and so he exaggerates to entertain her. He notices the sun in her pale red hair, how it stops against her yellow cardigan and her brown stockings. Too fair to tan. Everything about her fading.

You need a hat, he says.

The clouds above are ridged like the sand on the beach. Ripples and ridges reflected against light blue.

The ground is in the air, Leah says, pointing. The difference is, the sky's sand is white.

The warm grey beach smells like salt and decay. Wet seaweed, bullwhips wrapped around driftwood, pebbles caught in the slimy strands and yellow bulbs of the bullwhips and the dark green and brown of the seaweed. All left behind by the water when the tide went out for more.

Keeping an eye on her, Andy sat on a log with his

back to the sea and rolled a cigarette. She was never far from the bush by the tracks. Like a wild brown rabbit, she kept close to cover. You wouldn't catch her looking like some magazine picture walking across the sand with her dress blowing against her legs, thought Andy, her thinness the thinness of the air just about sweeping her up and away. Not likely. No wide open spaces for her, in spite of her being a prairie chicken.

Leah glanced at him rolling the cigarette. He saves his tobacco tins for nails, she knows. He carries nails in his mouth when his hands are full; when he isn't wearing his pouch, four or five nails stick out of his mouth.

The sea approaches and fills the thin, sharp line lovers have left making paths with sticks as they walked. Fills in the heart and the initials and the arrow.

Stubborn white trumpet flowers crawl up the granite boulders reaching for the rails, but then what? Blackberry barriers, steel tracks, crushed gravel. Trains.

Like blackberry bushes, Leah says low to herself. That's how I'd like to be. Strong, and safe. Bearing flowers, and fruit.

Pie *à la mode* and coffee at McBride's. A birthday treat. Cherry for Andy; raisin for Leah.

Andy is back at the doctor's house, in daylight this time, rain dripping from his hat, from his sleeves and bare hands.

She won't stop crying, Doctor, he says. I don't know what to do.

Is she taking her medication?
I think she flushed it down the toilet.
And nothing will calm her?
Nothing I can come up with.

So next is the hospital, Riverview.

Sleep tight, Leah, says Andy as he leaves her, goes home alone.

His morning coffee perks on the stove, oatmeal bubbles in a pot, bacon fat sputters in the pan. An imaginary Leah peeks out from behind the dusty curtains and smiles at him, at the honey dripping from his toast and down his chin.

One of the little girls from next door comes over after breakfast. Where's Mrs. Thompkins? she asks.

She's not here right now, says Andy. But you can stay if you like.

Okay, she says, and promptly launches into a story. In her closet she goes to the land of the fairies, she says. She likes to visit, she tells him, the way she likes to visit him, and Mrs. Thompkins. In Fairyland they have stuff called ambrosia, and stuff called Turkish delight. Does he have anything like that? And *where* is Mrs. Thompkins? she asks again.

He pours her a glass of apple juice. How about a song? he says. How about I teach you a song.

Sure, she says. What song?

From this valley they say you are going,
We will miss your bright eyes and sweet smile

For they say you are taking the sunshine
That has brightened our pathway a while

Three weeks later, Leah comes home. With a soft brush she cleans off the eggs as she sits on the porch's single step. Each egg must take her an hour. Her eyes are always cast down, and there is hesitation, doubt, in every motion she can bring herself to make.

She is so sad, Andy thinks, rolling himself a smoke, watching her from the shed. She is so goddamn sad. Mosquitoes just bite a little, like stinging nettles. Garter snakes? Nothing at all. But this, this is something different.

We can leave, Leah, Andy says. We can drive up north.

Where?

Past Hundred Mile, past Spuzzum, past Smithers, George, Rupert. Uranium is what we'd be after. I've been reading.

Her brown eyes dart, her hands tremble. The eggs, Andy. The mushrooms. No. The cat. We can't leave the cat.

Leah –

No. We can't.

Andy can't get the truck going. They'll miss Leah's appointment, and the doctor won't see her at home anymore. Inside the house, Leah doesn't care about the appointment. Slowly, she dusts her china dog collection. Sets each dog back in its place on the living-room windowsill. China dogs from boxes of tea, and fairs, and the five-to-a-dollar store on birthdays and Christmas. She dusts the three miniature teacups. She dusts the two *pysanky* eggs she brought from Saskatchewan.

They have nothing inside them, like me, she thinks.

She sets each of them carefully back in its place.

Nothing inside, she repeats. Hollow. Everything sucked out.

She goes to her sewing machine and crouches down. She treadles with her hands, treadles, her body bending into the motion of the machine. Push, push, make me go, push, push, let me go, push, push, push, push, push, push.

Then she rises, goes into the kitchen and sits at the table. She focuses on the patterns the mud-packed treads of Andy's boots have left on the flowered linoleum floor.

You've let the flowers get dirty again, she says to the quiet. Bad girl.

They don't get to town. Andy works some more on the truck. Walks over to the store for a new tin of tobacco. Sits on the truck's tailgate and rolls a smoke in the sun.

Inside the house, wooden kitchen chairs with rungs. Oilcloth on the table. Dusty cotton curtains. Big wood stove. Hay ropes looped over the back door's knob.

Leah carries the chair up the stairs to the attic.

Places the chair in the doorway.

She steps up, hay rope in hands.

Leah?

Andy carries her down the narrow attic stairs. He sits on the living-room couch beside her. Holds her cold hands, turns the wedding ring on her thin ring finger.

Around six-thirty he goes over to the doctor's. He can see the family through the dining-room window; he can see how the white Danish lampshade above the table reflects in all the windows like a moon. The doctor sits at the head of the table, his wife at the foot, the four girls, two on either side with their silverware gleaming, their legs swinging, their serviettes slipping and slipped from their laps. He knocks on the glass door. The irritated glance of the wife means go around to the proper door can't you see stupid man that it is dinnertime show a little common sense. *These people,* the doctor will be saying to his wife, may simply not know any better, Evelyn. And she will reply, I should be more gracious, I suppose, but heavenly day, *anyone* can know plain good manners.

I'm sorry to bother you, Andy mouths through the glass.

The doctor drops his white serviette on the table beside his place, leaves the table, and comes to the door.

I'm sorry to bother you...

The doctor turns his back to his family as if to protect them, steps outside into the evening. As the two men stand together talking on the cement patio, the doctor's body tenses, and for a brief instant his eyes dash wildly about as though looking for escape. Then they go hard and steady. Without a word to his wife, without a coat, the doctor follows Andy across the lawn, past the shadowy substance of the hanging baskets, and through the gate. Into Andy's misery. His despairing, despaired, and now dead wife, on the couch, covered with a quilt. Her head on the black and gold Niagara Falls pillow. "For My Wife, from Niagara Falls."

Not much can be done now, says the doctor. But you should call –

Sweet peas, or beans, on netting, thinks Andy, looking out the living-room window. Nope, a hummingbird in a net. Or that wild brown rabbit, scared to death, trying to hide in the grass, but the dog gets it.

Andy leaves the small stucco house on a Saturday morning. He goes over to the doctor's to say goodbye, walks around the long body of the house and to the back door and the buzzer.

Yes, Andy? says Mrs. Doctor, as kindly as she can.

Is the doctor home, says Andy.

One moment please, she says. She partially closes the door, and calls shrilly, Harry! It's Andy at the door.

The two men stand outside together, the doctor on the back porch, two hands on the railing, Andy on the sidewalk. When Andy turns to go, the doctor impulsively steps down and holds out his hand. Andy takes it.

Have a safe trip, Andy, says the doctor.

Thank you, says Andy.

Andy, I'm – It's all too bad, Andy. That things turned out this way.

Yes, says Andy.

And it's over. Andy walks home, closes the gate, climbs into the cab of his truck. He backs up, turns around, and drives down the puddled driveway. The camper sways as the truck forges heavily ahead, wetting the tires with its unsteady rhythm.

nobody's fool

*W*hen Luanne reached for little Booker across the kitchen table, he ducked under it. He ran through the door, and through the chicken wire gate, and out into the vegetable garden. Luanne sighed, reached for the coffee pot, refilled her mug. Added the milk and sugar and breathed deeply again, stirring. She rested her head in the cup of one hand and watched Booker as he hid behind the sunflowers and the compost. As lean as a stalk, he is, like his father.

Behind her on the fridge are two postcards from that father. Apparently still sunning it up in California. Both cards have pictures of Carmel. Caramel, says Booker. Luanne's husband, or what used to pass for a husband, as she says wryly to the few friends and neighbours she has in her arsenal, has been to California several times now in the last six months. The previous six months, it was Colorado. Something American appealing to him.

Or someone. Business, he says, objecting to her innu-
endoes. Right, Brad, she retorts. Business. He didn't
come home, come here, between his trips; on her
request, he stayed in the city, with friends. Called from
there to see if he could come to see them.

See Booker, she said.

See you and Booker, he said.

Whatever. Come out if you want. We'll be here.

The big dog's fur is warm under her feet. You are my
furry black footstool, Chester, she tells him silently. And
lie just as still. Maybe I will stuff you when you are
dead. How would you like that? The dog shifts slightly,
snores gently. His tail twitches. You are snoring, she tells
him out loud, and he stops. Ah, for a man like this, she
thinks, and rubs his belly with her toes.

But she's had it with men. Starting with Brad.

I see you, Booker, she says softly to her small son, but
he doesn't hear her. I see your red shoes, she calls more
loudly, aiming her voice out the door. Booker's red runners move immediately, lift up one by one as he takes
them off. He flings them toward the door but they don't
quite make it, land with thumps against the wall, one
and two, in the flowering mint by the wooden steps.

She's feeling relatively calm today. In that brief lull
between the end of her period and the beginning of
PMS. By tomorrow or the next day, she will be back to
feeling there is too much she can do nothing about. Too
much sadness in the world. Too many animals exploit-
ed, abused, starved to death. All the world's rivers, too
polluted to drink from. The pregnant girls and women
in Rwanda, fetuses cut from their bellies after the gang

rapes. The child prostitutes in Brazil. The world is too full of pain, some days, for her to cope with, and she cries, sometimes with guilt and sometimes with help-lessness. If the gulls with the plastic pop rings around their necks starve, what can she do about it? Nothing. If children are fucked and strangled, what can she do? Nothing.

Join something, Brad said many times. Volunteer at the SPCA.

She didn't. It seemed too small an act, a drop in the bucket. Oh how could she have brought someone as precious as Booker into such a world?

What choice is there, said Brad. What other world could you bring a child into?

Shut up, Brad. Just shut up, would you?

Once her period starts, she regains some sense of control. She feels again that maybe she *can* do some-thing, at least for Booker. Here at home. And so she tries to keep the bad from him, determined that he should know, for as long as possible, only joy. She does much of her crying in secret. She puts the newspapers on the top shelf of the bookcase. She listens to the eleven o'clock news when Booker is in bed asleep. She gives the TV away to the Sally Ann.

You're being overly protective, Luanne, Brad says. You're not giving him the real world when you do that. At school he'll learn about the starving children in Ethiopia. About the war in Yugoslavia. Better the real thing instead of Darth Vader, don't you think?

Drop it, Brad. You're not a parent around here any-more.

Chester was a tiny puppy when she got him, but he grew like crazy right from the start. And did he cry. Incessantly. He whimpered when she shut him out of the bathroom; when he was hungry, which was almost always; when, for the first couple of months, he couldn't climb up on her bed; when she took a man into her bed and kicked Chester out. Chester wanted to be with her more than any place on earth. Ah, for a man like that, she thinks again. Fuck you, Mr. On-the-Road-to-California.

When she first brought Booker's father here, Chester looked as though his heart would break. And much later, in fact years later, three days after Booker came home from the hospital with Luanne, the dog went out and lay in the farthest corner of the garden, curled up against the corner post in the tomato plants. He knew full well the garden was off limits. He flattened himself as much as he could into the earth. She called him and called him. He wouldn't come. In the end she went out to him, lowered herself down in the dirt beside him and stroked his long silky body, crooned her love for him. Sadly, he reached his nose up and sniffed her milky breasts. When finally he got up, there was a nest of tomatoes under him, punctured green tomatoes that he had pulled off the vines with his teeth. He reluctantly left the tomatoes and followed her back inside, where he acknowledged the baby's existence for the first time by sniffing his foot, then lay down under the kitchen table, his nose against the leg of Luanne's chair. Not long after, he fell in love with Booker.

Chester went on to become the only living creature

in the house who was not affected in some negative way by the exit of Booker's father just over a year ago. The moment Brad left the property, Chester was more mellow in temperament. He stopped shoving his nose hard between people's legs when they came to visit, stopped pushing his way into every room ahead of Luanne to stand there whining vigorously with misplaced hope – habits she had tried to break in him in every way she could think of while Brad was still here. And the dog's coat became glossier, the feathers on his legs and tail silkier. The head male of the house, restored to his rightful position.

Luanne, however, was not more mellow when Brad left. Frightened, furious, she was wired for days. So unhappy she wished she'd die. It was hell. Chester's whining and wagging. Her crying. The ingenuous concern on Booker's face, the sweet blankness which covered his confusion and uncertainty. The misery and anger on Brad's face as he slammed the car door and pulled away.

In Luanne's version, she and Brad went from fire in the belly to baby in the belly in just over a year. Then there were a few more turbulent years before half-burned, charred ends and ashes were what remained in an otherwise empty grate. No one interested in stirring the ashes or taking the time to blow on them.

I should have called Booker Phoenix, thinks Luanne. The only beauty to come out of all that. The only thing worth saving. That much is obvious. Bastard, she says to the mantel, where she knows a picture of Brad lies face down behind a Chinese tea chest.

Booker is ambushing something in the sunflowers. Maybe another two weeks or a month, and then the flowers will open, and they'll be gorgeous. Right now their big green heads droop coyly. Booker crawls slowly at their feet, pauses stock-still, looks around, then gradually moves forward once again. He's been watching the neighbour's barn cat hunt again, has been practising her moves.

What are you stalking, Booker? Luanne wonders quietly, tapping her spoon on the side of her coffee mug. And will the techniques you are developing serve you later in life? Lazily, she digs her toes deep into Chester's black fur, can feel his rib cage under all that softness. He's getting old, poor fellow. Older. Aren't we all? she says to him. He thumps his tail against the floor. That's my boy. Good dog.

Chester is content with concentrating on domestic details these days, and unlike her, he is content with simply being content. She sighs. There are still several miles to go, and several memories to take care of, before this elusive perfect happiness makes an appearance that could last.

We're going to make cookies, Luanne calls after another few seconds, and waits. There are one or two certainties around here, and the response she expects now is one of them. Simultaneously and instantly, Booker casts off his hunter's stance and runs in. Chester scrambles out from under the table. The two of them stand, expectant and happy, in front of her. My boys, she says, waving her teaspoon at them. I can count on you, can't I? Now, your lazy mama is going to get up and get productive, and you're going to help her, aren't you?

Luanne and Booker pick peas in the garden. Chester lies in the shade on the porch, where they will join him, once the shelling begins. Move over, big fella, Luanne will say. Give us some room. And Chester will lazily roll over onto his other side, and she and Booker will sit down and hang their legs over the wooden porch, and separate the peas from the pods, peas in one bowl and pods in the other, mix them up sometimes, and decide what to have with the peas for their supper. Biscuits, Booker will say. Cheese. Tomatoes. Milk. Peanut butter cookies.

But a car pulls into the driveway and changes all that.

It is dark green, classy, if a bit old, a 1975 Lincoln Town Car. There is a man inside, a man in a white Stetson.

Alberta, says Luanne. Or Texas. I wonder why.

Calgary Stampede, says Booker.

That's your father in that car, says Luanne.

My father! says Booker.

He didn't call ahead, says Luanne. Just look at us. The Grubbola triplets.

Chester rises with a stretch, growls low and long. Though his tail wags, it wags gently enough to change its mind.

He remembers this guy, Luanne supposes, and his feelings are mixed. Mine too, Chester, she tells him silently. Chester looks up at her.

Howdy there, pardner, Brad says, getting out of the car and approaching. Pardner and ma'am, I suppose I should say. Guess where I've been?

I don't want to know, says Luanne. Let the suspense kill me.

You're as funny as ever, aren't you, Lulu? Your mama, she's a lulu, Booker T.

Now Booker is out in the yard with his new bug house, gathering grass and weeds for the bugs to eat. There won't be much room for bugs pretty soon, he thinks. Or they'd better be good and hungry. He giggles. His father brought him this present from Nevada. That's where he's been. As he held it out to Booker with a golden brown hand, he said, I'm more ready for this bug house than you are, Booker T, but I think you'd better have it.

Booker's mother is inside the house crying. Booker can hear her. She has cried before, he remembers. Especially that one time. He went up to her and asked, What is the matter? And when she didn't answer, he touched her on the knee.

Oh, something awful happened in Saskatoon, she said then, putting a warm, cupped hand on his head. Bad men killed seven cocker spaniels. They beat them to death with two-by-fours. Luanne began to sob. Three of them were puppies. Why do you think they did that, Booker? What the hell was the point?

I don't know, said Booker, troubled.

I don't know why either, she said. But it makes me so sad I can hardly stand it.

Me too, said Booker.

Booker doesn't know why she's crying now. His father has been gone about an hour, but that's not why she's sad; he knows that she is glad that he has gone – she tells him that every time his father leaves. Booker shakes the grass and leaves out of his bug house and puts it down. Wanders into the house to find something else to do.

Inside the house Luanne is face down on her bed whispering through clenched teeth. You bastard you bastard you bastard. On the floor beside the bed is the whitest chenille dressing gown she has ever seen, with satin piping, satin pockets, and a chocolate smear on one sleeve. On the bed beside her foot is a box of Godiva chocolates. Four are missing. She feels the box against her toe and kicks it onto the floor. She hears the chocolates tumble out.

She had asked him straight out. Why did you bring me this dressing gown, Brad? What do you want?

He tipped his Stetson back on his head. Wiped the sweat from the creases on his brow. I don't want anything. It's just a present.

Yes, you do so want something. What is it?

Okay. I want understanding. Always have, always will.

Sorry. Fresh out.

I want you, Luanne.

You should have thought of that before.

Luanne, nothing happened.

Right.

Nothing has ever happened. In all this time.

Right.

Luanne is putting cooled cookies into tins. Six dozen less a couple of handfuls. Whose full hands? Hers, and Booker's. She is nobody's fool. She will be nobody's fool even if it means she will be nobody's. Chester is out in the yard, at the horse trough where no horses drink; he's slurping long, cool swallows of artesian well water through lush green grass growing tall around the concrete trough. Lapping and lapping Chester drinks, noisy and sloppy. Now he ambles off, shaking water from his jowls. He lifts his leg absentmindedly and pees long against the telephone pole in the yard, then marches, replete, relieved, and happy, tail high and wagging wide, back across the drive to the porch. Halfway there, he lies down in the dust and rolls. Groans with pleasure. How does one reach such a state of self-sufficiency? Luanne wonders. Chester is happy. He knows how to make himself happy. And he's a frigging dog.

Booker is lying on his bed with his library book on gorillas. On the shelf above his bed is the bug house. He emptied it out and put it there last week, and hasn't done more than look at it since. After awhile, he puts down his book, lifts his hands up in front of him and the light falls on them. His arms are in shadow; his hands are in light. He likes that. Does it again. Again. Look, he says. Come see. But it doesn't really matter that his mother can't hear him. He likes this himself. Look, he says again. Look and see. Okay, he answers. Show me. Then he makes some shadow pictures, jaws from his small hands. That's pretty neat, he says, and laughs. Then he makes a shadow picture of a gun with his thumb and first finger. He plays for a few seconds, then says, Mummy wouldn't like that one.

This week in Uganda bad people killed three gorillas. Three members of a gorilla family who lived in a special park in the jungle where they are supposed to be safe. Bang bang bang.

Mummy? What is this a picture of?

Oh Booker. It is a picture of dead gorillas.

Dead? Why?

Oh Booker.

Booker looks at the picture of a baby gorilla nursing. Kisses the gorillas good night and good morning as though this will save them.

Chester, lying by the door, whimpers in a bad dream, cries out with meek yelps.

It's okay, Chester, calls Booker. It's okay, good dog. Chester half opens one eye, closes it again. Thumps his tail once, sighs, and sleeps clear. Booker climbs down from his bed and goes over to him. He kneels down, strokes Chester's muzzle and where his eyebrows might be. Lifts his silky ears and looks inside. Lifts his lips.

His lips are like black rubber, says Booker. And would you look at his teeth! Chester lies still, eyes dreamily watching.

You be kind to all animals, his mother has told him. Always.

Why?

Because it is the right thing to do.

Are people animals?

Yes, Booker, people are animals. Except that some are mean just to be mean. Other animals don't do that.

Luanne is writing a letter at the kitchen table. Please, it says. Please what? she asks herself. Please fuck right off and don't come near me again because I can't resist you, you bastard? She feels as though she has been writing this letter for years.

I thought it was the kindest way, he said.

Liar, she said. Despicable, sonofabitching liar.

I didn't lie, he said. I just didn't tell you. I thought it was what you wanted.

Get out, she said. Go away.

All right, he said. But let me tell you this: if you think happiness can be found sitting on this goddamn joke of a farm all by yourself, you're nuts. It would come from our being together. If you would let us. If you would quit the martyr act and believe me.

There isn't a choice, Brad. There is simply the right thing to do.

Luanne —

No.

When he led her into the bedroom with the box of chocolates, sent Booker outside to catch some bugs, put the box on the bed, and turned to her. When he did that, she felt hunger rise like heartburn. Fast and painful and hot. Luanne, he said. I brought you something.

Why? she said. Don't you come near me.

I don't know, he said, coming near her. I saw this and was able, for a change, to buy you something really nice. Do you like it?

And then he kissed her in the hollow above her collarbone. That kiss his stun gun, and he knew it. Then he kissed her ever so lightly all along her collarbone, and down between her breasts. There was no going back after that. Back to her promise to herself last time that she would shove him away the next time he tried this on her. Lonely, hungry, her body failed her again.

I want to see this on you, he whispered.

No.

Come on. Just for a minute.

Booker –

Booker's outside. He's busy. See?

Out the bedroom window, Booker crouched in the dust, holding something between his thumb and forefinger. Intense concentration on his face and in his body.

Luanne is at the kitchen table again, this time with her chemistry text open before her. She has spent three years so far working towards this degree. At this rate, there are about seven more years ahead. Booker will be a teenager. To be even halfway through would mean so much. One course, two courses a year. Last year summer school, Booker in the trailer, parked in a rented driveway near the campus with a sitter, Chester cramped and miserable on a chain, sleeping in the dust underneath. What they do for her, she thinks. Without question they adapt. So willingly. So full of generous love.

Her own love is not so generous, she suspects. She has always found it difficult to reciprocate in matters of the heart. Has guarded herself closely, especially suspicious in the face of what appears to be unconditional love. How could anyone love, or love her, like that? Suspecting, perhaps, that she wouldn't survive the trauma if her love were rejected. Give up on them before they give up on you.

Booker sits at the table with his head on his arms; he's drawing large birds with wax crayons. Luanne looks up from her textbooks and watches him. She remembers the first time she saw that sweet head emerging from between her legs, saw the wet dark hair on his scalp. Even though she had been carrying him around in her body all those months, and had seen him more than once on the ultrasound screen, he hadn't become real until then. She still remembers the amazement she felt, a kind of awe. There's a human being coming out of me. This *human being* is being born. Look, Brad. Look!

That is a large black cloud you're drawing there, Booker, Luanne says. Will the sun come out, do you suppose, or is it going to rain?

That is not a cloud, Mummy. That is Chester.

Ah. Silly me, B.

But yes, it is going to rain. Outside. Look.

There are indeed dark clouds in the sky. Many of them.

Tears fill her eyes. Oh, hell. Tears come too easily these days.

She digs her toes deeper into Chester's fur and bursts into tears.

What's wrong, Mummy? says Booker, worried.

I need a walk, says Luanne. Do you know anyone who would go for a walk in the rain?

Luanne and Booker stand in yellow slickers by the door. Chester is smelly; he shakes water all over the walls. Drops of water sizzle as they hit the potbelly stove. Wet faces, dry feet in gumboots slick with red-brown mud.

You go on back outside, Chester, Luanne says. You are too smelly right now. Stay on the porch and keep dry. Good dog.

Chester wags his tail in response, then waits for the door to open, and goes out.

Mum? says Booker a little while later. What do you do when there's nothing you can do?

Like when?

Like the gorillas. Dying.

I don't know. Let it hurt. Hope it will go away. Think about what makes you happy. Maybe that would help. What makes you happy, Booker?

Gorillas. And Chester. And the baby fish that we watched being born when Daddy still lived here. Remember?

Yes. Did you know, Booker, that I watched you being born?

Really? Booker smiles.

It's pretty exciting when a new human being is born.

It's pretty exciting when *anything* is being born, says Booker. But especially me, right?

Later still, Booker is lying on his back on the rug, flying folded paper through the air.

When I was inside you, was I afraid of anything?

No, says Luanne. You weren't afraid. You were safe and warm.

I get afraid now, says Booker. Sometimes.

What are you afraid of, my love?

I'm not sure.

Try not to be afraid, she says. I will look after you the best I can. So will Chester.

I know, says Booker. It's just –

I know.

Hey, Booker, says Luanne. Do you know where Chester is?

No.

I haven't seen him in ages. He's not on the porch.

He went outside in the rain. Maybe he got lost.

I hope not. I hope he is warm and dry somewhere. He must be hungry for his supper.

The next afternoon a small flatbed truck comes up the driveway. Parks by the water trough. Luanne steps out onto the porch. Loves the after-the-rain smell of the air. Wishes Chester were here to stand beside her. A man calls from the cab of the truck, Is the boy around? She nods but signals him to whisper; Booker fell asleep while looking at his book. The man nods and slowly pulls the truck closer. She recognizes him; he lives up the road. The man gets out, eases his door shut.

I'm sorry, he says.

It's okay, she says. He probably won't wake up.

No, he said, tipping his cap back. That's not what I mean. He rubs his forehead. I'm *sorry*. And his eyes glance back toward the flatbed of his truck.

Luanne sees wet black fur.

Found your dog, says the man. In the ditch by my place. Brought him back to you.

Chester.

Hit, I thought at first. But no. Shot. Don't know who'd do that around here.

Shot.

Where do you want me to put him?

I don't know. Just take him down first, would you please? Gently?

You bet. I've got him on an old blanket here.

The man lifts Chester off the truck. Luanne kneels in the turnaround beside the body of her dog. She rocks in her own arms, cries over the body of this animal who has meant so much to her for so long. Strokes his beautiful black fur, wet with rain and blood, touches the worn pads of his still paws. How she has loved this dog. How he has given so selflessly his entire life, and always with love in his eyes. And the last time she saw him she sent him back out into the rain.

Chester! comes Booker's voice from the porch. There you are, bad dog! Where have you been?

That night Luanne lies on her bed, rests her hands on her belly. What will she do without Chester? Her own, her beloved. Later that night she dreams she gives birth to a puppy that is clearly Chester when he was small. He emerges from her, slips wet and vulnerable and black from her body, and she cradles him in her arms and against her chest. He nuzzles against her, cries puppy cries, licks her breast with his tiny pink tongue.

Booker is down at the pond, playing at fishing. Mud squishes up between his bare feet, mosquitoes linger on his tender arms. Chester is not on the bank near him, not asleep on moist dark earth in the tall grass, hiding his nose from mosquitoes.

Luanne had wondered from time to time what she would do if Brad died. If Booker died. When she thought those thoughts, her heart contracted with such fear she couldn't breathe. But never Chester. She had never thought that he would die, never really considered it for an instant. He would always be her dog. Period.

Where have you been, bad doggy? Booker had exclaimed *when he reached the flatbed truck.*

Booker, said Luanne, Chester has died.

Died?

We have to bury him now. Maybe you could help me.

What is this world coming to? Luanne says aloud to no one.

And then she replies, The world has always been full of this, Luanne, and you know it.

Luanne stands among the blackberry fronds coated in thorns. Thick prickles barb into clothes, under runners, against legs. Lift this arch of bramble, duck under here. One – *ouch* – caught in her scalp. Beads of blood, beads of blackberry juice. Plump black fruit smells juicy in the sun, in her mouth, plunks in the yellow plastic bucket. She stands, caught, immobilized by the arms of thorns, while her son plays contentedly in the water; her man drives through another country; and her dog, Chester, is dead.

There is black dirt thick under her nails from burying him. Chester was a big dog, and she had to dig a big, deep hole. She was able to carry his body, still wrapped in the blanket, to the edge of the hole, and from there, she rolled it in. Then she covered him up with earth while Booker stood at some distance, watching solemnly. He didn't start to cry until she tamped down the mound with the back of the shovel. He came over then, and crouched down beside the grave. So, then, did she, and together they patted the earth over Chester with their hands.

indelible *marks*

*b*efore Rose leaves for work, and then once, twice, or three times during the evening, she likes to sit with a big mug of tea and watch Channel Four, the text news station, go all the way around: National Headlines, Regional Headlines, Business News, Entertainment Highlights, Sports, and Lotto Numbers. She knows this pastime is a little unusual, but for her, staring at the monotonous, fluorescent text constitutes a kind of meditation. It removes her from the world. She finds that soothing.

This morning on the Regional Headlines she read a story about a man who ran into a burning house to save his dog. Now the man, a Mr. Robinson, is in the burn unit at the hospital in Edmonton, and almost dead. His dog died in the fire. All morning Rose has been composing a letter to the man, and the letter has interfered with her getting her work done because it keeps taking over her head. It's a good thing that she's practically the boss. Dear Mr. Robinson. I am deeply moved and impressed by your courage when you ran into the fire to try to save your dog. Not many people are so brave. You are exceptional. You are admirable. I will remember you and your act of love and courage for a long time. Please get better soon.

During lunch hour, she leaves her desk to pop across the street to the Bay, to buy Mr. Robinson a card. What kind of card does one send in such a situation? She pauses for a second as she ponders this question, and that's when she glances over into the Bay's Mirror Room and sees Elsa. Elsa, shopping. Rose can hardly believe it's her. Except that there is no mistaking that profile. That nose, that forehead – distinctively, charmingly, Elsa. Without thinking, Rose ducks behind a pillar by the escalator. From there she watches Elsa leaf through the designer clothes. It appears she is just finishing with Alfred Sung, and is moving towards Jones New York.

When Rose knew Elsa in the Windermere Valley a decade ago, Elsa lived in a small log cabin in Dry Gulch. Rose sat in that cabin many times, eating garbanzo bean loaf and brown rice, drinking herbal tea. Sometimes they sat cross-legged on Elsa's futon, sipping Southern Comfort and orange juice, dribbling small handfuls of home-grown pot down the covers of record albums to sort out the seeds; Rose rolled joints they smoked while listening to Doc Watson, Linda Ronstadt, Emmylou Harris. The cabin, Rose remembers, had a small wood heater, powder blue walls, and cabinets the colour of orange sherbet. Teaspoons had been nailed on the cupboard doors to serve as handles. There was an outhouse, and a small stream out back from which the cold running water came. Elsa lived in this cabin with a cat named Moonbeam.

There were a lot of hippies in the Valley in those days. They lived in teepees out in the woods, in cabins, or in rented houses in small nearby communities like Edgewater, Spillimacheen, or Radium. Rose was one of them, though she never felt sure she belonged. She was never, she thought, completely a hippie, though she did live in a teepee about three miles from town. She had a car, for one thing, a 1963 Volkswagen bug, and she had a steady job, waitressing. Most of the others did not work, or worked only long enough to collect UIC, and so they were better able to be organic in their approach to life than she.

Rose was nineteen. She had left the coast and come to the Valley to escape her mother, who likely hadn't noticed she'd gone. Her critical, angry mother, whose fury periodically and unpredictably descended upon Rose like a blanket flung over her head. The rest of the time Rose didn't exist. Now all that would change. She was free. She could do whatever she wanted.

Rose and the other hippies shared the one hotel bar with small-time loggers, local business, and a handful of Natives from the nearby reserve. Most evenings, many of the hippies could be found drinking draft and shooting pool. Often they were high on pot, sometimes on acid, and generally they were mellow, and laid-back. They drove their pickup trucks, or walked, or hitchhiked into town, and always ended up at the National Park Hotel.

In a subtle, sensuous way, Elsa Moore was the belle of the bar. At closing time you'd see her, gently reeling, smiling sweetly, as she climbed into a pickup, or an old van, with whoever she'd been eyeing that night. Elsa had her pick; everyone wanted to sleep with her. She was beautiful in a way uniquely hers – she had long, black, silky hair, and freckles, and clear, pale blue, flirty eyes. A way of moving that made you think of sex because of the way her braless breasts rhythmically touched the cloth of her light peasant blouses, the way her skirts swished as she walked, her movements graceful even in her steel-toed workboots.

You seldom saw Elsa with men during the day; she said with a smile that she saved them for the night. The day belonged to her women companions, was for embroidering jackets, mending and modifying clothes purchased at the thrift store, making bead and wire and feather earrings, baking, doing laundry at the laundromat. During the summer, Rose and Elsa lay together topless in the sun outside Elsa's cabin, lay with one hand up to protect squinting eyes from the bright sun as the joints passed back and forth. Summer in the Valley. Planting gardens; drinking mint tea; talking about men.

I'd like to do that Clive, Elsa might say with a mischievous soft smile. Anybody know anything about him?

Didn't know him before he came here.

That's not what I mean.

They all laughed.

I've done him, someone else might say. But I don't remember much.

That says something.

They laughed again.

How about Earl? someone said one day.

The laughter stopped.

Let's not talk about Earl, said Elsa. I was having fun.

Who's Earl? Rose asked.

Don't ask. You don't want to know.

Maybe a night or two later, Elsa would go off to do the man of choice, whoever he was. Always a little, sometimes a lot, drunk; always just once, sometimes twice, and then there'd be no one for a few nights, and then it would be someone else, someone new, or someone she hadn't done for some time.

As they picked up their buckskin jackets, their work vests, their heavy flannel shirts, as they finished off the last of their draft, pouring half into a friend's glass, as they rolled a joint for the road and bought a case of off-sale, as they picked up their pouches of Drum tobacco and their rolling papers, as they made one last trip to the can, Elsa flitted, in one way or another, through all the men's minds.

The way she moved late at night made you imagine her hair coming loose of its braid; imagine her blouse being lifted up over her breasts and pulled over her head; imagine her skirt hiked up past her thighs as she lay on her back, knees up, wool socks around her ankles, workboots flung in a corner by the wood stove.

Rose adored Elsa, for Elsa was everything Rose was afraid to be. Sensual. Promiscuous. Comfortable in her body so that her moods and desires were evident in her flesh. When she was angry, when she was happy – she didn't need words. Her body told you. Standing at the pool table with three men, an observer could tell which one she was interested in by the subtle pull of her body towards him. It was amazing, really. Rose watched her with envy, and with love.

Rose felt privileged to be Elsa's friend. But she felt undeserving, too – Rose carried lessons from her mother, and felt herself ugly, and odd. *What's the matter with you, anyway?* her mother would say. Though when she searched in the mirror for her deformities, Rose couldn't see what was so bad. *Her* body didn't tell her a thing; she figured it had nothing to tell her worth hearing.

These bad feelings either heightened when she was near Elsa, or vanished altogether. The latter times were joyful: for their duration, she felt as sexy and desirable as Elsa was. Rose tossed her braids back, she loosened her hips, she leaned over the pool table to make shots the way Elsa did, ways that revealed, She felt the way Elsa felt: assured, fond of herself; open. But still she knew she felt this only on her surface, while Elsa felt it all the way through. Elsa was the real thing; you could tell just by looking at her.

Sometimes when they were together, Rose felt like they were playing dolls, and she was Elsa's doll. Elsa dressed Rose up in her clothes, in her skirts and blouses; she played with her hair, and then took her to the bar to show her off. One afternoon they had stayed at the cabin and smoked some hash, and Rose was sitting at the kitchen table while Elsa brushed her long brown hair. She was going to plait it into little braids, inserting decorations of feathers, and bind the ends of the braids with pieces of rawhide. Rose loved the feel of Elsa's hands on her head, loved Elsa being close. She had been allowing her thoughts to just drift, but then she snapped to when Elsa said something about "when I'm married and have kids."

Is that what you want? asked Rose, surprised. Is that *all?* Married with kids?

Sure. I like kids.

I don't. I want to go to school.

I was never very good at school.

But you're smart! We could go together.

I'm not smart at school stuff. Nope. I just want to marry somebody with lots of money and stay home and have some kids. But not yet. And then she laughed. Too much to *do,* first, she said. Maybe when I'm twenty-five. Before I get wrinkles.

I'm going to school. Eventually. My mother wants me to go. In her letters she always asks me when I'm going. Maybe when she stops bugging me about it I'll actually go.

When Earl walked into the beer parlour one night, home from working up north, his arrival stirred as much energy as Elsa's did, but there was something more ominous than exciting in the air. In those days Rose couldn't tell the difference. The air crackled. He exuded some kind of danger. It caught her attention.

Who's that? she asked Elsa.

A jerk you don't want to know, Elsa replied.

How do you know? Rose persisted. Have you done him?

No. I'd never do him.

There was something about him, Rose thought. Something exciting. Different. Maybe Elsa was afraid, thought Rose. And like a boy riding a Brahma bull just to show he can, she took Earl on as soon as he made a clumsy, drunken pass at her.

Rose does more before and after work than stare at Channel Four. The last few months she's been watching the American election, as well. Ross Perot, Bill Clinton, George Bush. Each night she has watched the primaries on US cable, watched the clips about the candidates' wives, children, pets. Why? She hasn't the foggiest idea. And on weekend nights, she sits in front of her TV and VCR watching a rented movie, with a bowl of popcorn and a Big Rock ale on the small table in front of her, and the controls in her lap. Occasionally, as she sits there, she wonders what the people in the office would make of her life outside work if they knew what went on. What didn't go on, is more like it. When she goes home. What home means to her. Her Mr. Submarine wrappers. Her cans of Campbell's hearty soups. This fine old house, and her small, but certain, presence in it.

When she comes into her house each night after work, the hardwood floors gleam; the air, freshly pumped through the air cleaner, smells almost sweet. This house is the house of her dreams. Real leaded windows. Old, well-maintained hardwood floors. A claw-footed bathtub. A security system. She is safe here.

But in some moments, particularly in the winter, as she stands kicking off her boots in the foyer, as she picks up her mail – mostly bills, and the rare letter from her still unvanquished mother – she has longed for something, has longed for there to be someone to meet her at the door, offer warmth. It would be nice to be less self-sufficient sometimes, she thinks; for the responsibility for herself not to fall so completely upon her own shoulders. And on these days, the days when her life is not enough, she comes close to tears. Yet this is what she really wanted, she tells herself.

I want to belong to someone, she had yearned back then in those Valley days before she met Earl. If only I had a guy, she'd thought. Sometimes, she was surprised to discover that she even actually missed the heat of her mother's rage. What passed for caring. I want to matter, she'd cried to herself and the sky, feeling alone and abandoned, even though it was she who had run away from home. I want to *be* someone's. Well, she got what she wanted, that's for sure, when she got involved with Earl.

The very few boys and men who had touched Rose had done so drunkenly, rapidly, seeking only to enter and ejaculate. She didn't know how to ask for what she wanted because she had no idea what that was. She had never touched herself. But somewhere along the way she had decided there was something wrong with her, that she was malformed, that her clitoris didn't work. What

Earl did with his fat stubby fingers and that foul mouth came with the force of a revelation: she believed he wrought miracles. He changed her life.

She was to hold perfectly still when they had sex. Not move a muscle while he explored her, stroked her, poked her here, and here. Until she trembled and moaned as she came. And that, that coming, was like being swept up into heaven, and sometimes she wept in gratitude.

What Earl liked was to pin her down. Spread her legs. Bend her over the kitchen sink, say, her hands in the soapy water, while he fucked her.

You like this, don't you? Eh? Don't fucking *move*, I said. There. Earl made you feel good, didn't he? Now get me a fucking drink.

I don't like it when you talk to me like that, Earl.

If you don't like it, you know where the door is.

Earl, please –

You know where the door is.

The first time Earl hit her, she was more surprised than anything. Surprised that the blow was both new and old, familiar and unfamiliar. Same anger, different delivery. Though her mother was adept at both, she had generally preferred verbal to physical assaults. Out of the blue she would fling her angry words over Rose. *I don't know why I waste my time on you, you worthless numbskull. Can't you get anything through that thick head of yours?* But maybe it was better than nothing.

Rose stayed with Earl, month after month, though he

continued to hit her, eventually to beat her. Whenever she saw her, Elsa urged her to leave. But Rose couldn't explain the peculiar sense of power she seemed to have with Earl – how astonishing she found it that someone as inconsequential as she could evoke such an intense response in someone as clearly consequential as him. Stir him to such violent, passionate acts. *Cunt-face. Fucking cunt-face.* It was like a foreign language. As she looked at her uncertain, ingenuous face peering out from photographs taken back then. At her naive brown eyes, wide open. As she surveyed her tense, thin body, her tight little mouth. As she remembered her growing silence. As she lay there, bruised from his boots. Joints aching from his twisting her limbs. I give. I give in. Swear to God PLEASE you're hurting me I SAID PLEASE.

Late one night, when the bar was just closing, Earl laid into Rose for talking too long to the bartender when she went up to buy the off-sales. Earl twisted her arm up behind her back, steered her toward his black truck.

You're hurting me Earl. Please let go. Let go of me.

Shut up.

You're hurting me.

Shut the fuck up.

You're hurting her, *Earl.* The way Elsa said his name made it sound like a rock she had hurled. That hit him between the shoulder blades and stopped him. Elsa was coming out of the bar with Clive.

You *slime*ball. Leave her alone. Get away from her Earl, or you'll wish you had. I mean it.

Earl looked at Elsa. Spat. Let go of Rose's braid. Rose knelt on the asphalt.

You think you're so shit hot, don't you, Elsa? Earl said drunkenly.

Elsa stood pointing at him, one hand on her hip. Get out of here Earl, she said. You fucking get out of here *now*.

Earl swayed slightly as he looked at Elsa long and hard. He spat again. Then he walked up to her and said, I know where you live.

Go to hell, Earl, Elsa said. You go right to hell.

Earl bumped her hard with his shoulder as he went past her and into the bar.

You've got to stop it, Rose, Elsa said as she helped her to her feet. Elsa was shaking. Stop him. Do you hear me?

Yes. I know. Thank you, Rose said. Thank you, Elsa.

He's a total fucker.

I know.

She saw less of Elsa after that. Earl said he didn't like Rose seeing her. All you need is me, Rosie, he said, licking the inside of her ear. I'll be all you'll ever need.

Glenn Gould plays Bach behind the Channel Four news text. She smiles: it's quite the change from Doc Watson and Emmylou. She loves listening to Gould: his touch is so beautiful, so precise, and certain. When the piece ends, Rose aims the control at the TV and clicks it off. Listens to the silence, then to her voice in the silence.

I will look after you, house, she says. I will clean your eavestroughs. I will not let your roof leak. I will tend your grounds, I will weed your beds. I have entered into a relationship with you, house, and you will be able to count on me always. I am here for you, and you are here for me.

The injuries Earl inflicted upon Rose had grown progressively worse. Last time it was two broken fingers. The time before, three broken ribs. At first the brushes with danger had made her feel electrically, vibrantly alive. Now they just made her feel sad. Limp, and worn out, like the dishrag he called her. Her mother was right. Earl was right. She was a loathsome thing, and she was sick of her self-pity, and sick of playing, over and over again, the eight-track tape of Jim Croce's songs about martyrs and love gone wrong. Reality was flat and ugly. There was no romance in any of this. She mourned her past, her present, and whatever lay ahead.

Earl came home from the bar just before dawn in late October and told Rose how Elsa had "met her match" the night before, somewhere between the hotel and home.

So, Rosie, said Earl, yawning. Looks like someone put your pal Elsa in her place.

What do you mean?

Gave her the old one two. Gave her a piece of tail she didn't want. Cut that pretty face of hers, too.

Who? Earl, *who?*

Don't look at *me.* You sound like a fucking owl. How

the fuck would I know? One of those losers she picks up in the bar.

Someone *raped* her?

She probably had it coming to her.

How do *you* know about it? Who told you?

Guy at the gas station.

Rose was stunned, and frightened. Elsa, who had always seemed invincible, protected by goddesses. Rose didn't go to see her. She told herself she didn't know what to say. Elsa left the Valley within a couple of days and didn't come back – her parents came down from Edmonton and packed up her stuff and took her home. And then, within a couple of weeks, Rose did what Elsa had done: she left.

Rose lived in basement suites at first, because that was all she could afford. She didn't have much; she had left nearly everything, including her teepee, in the Valley. Now her jeans, her underwear, her T-shirts, her couple of sweaters sat on a shelf made from bricks and boards. A pillow, a sleeping bag opened up as a quilt over a set of sheets tucked around the single foamy on the floor. A clock radio with a broken radio. Three cups. Five glasses. A jar of instant coffee. Four spoons, five forks, and three knives, one of them sharp. In the fridge, milk. For the coffee. A carton of cigarettes. Ice cubes. Bottles of wine or spaces where the bottles of wine used to be. Cards and postcards she had bought or been sent taped on the cupboard doors. One can of mushroom and one of tomato soup. Some restaurant packages of sugar and coffee whitener.

She had borrowed money from her mother on the promise she would go to school. She spent her time studying, writing papers, reading the required books. She hunkered down, kept utterly to herself.

She has done very well in the ten years since she left the Valley. Very well indeed.

At night Rose stares at the off-white walls of her house until she is sucked empty of definition. Then she goes to bed. There, alone, she lies still, as he told her to do. Sometimes she can remember the feel of his mouth on her. His finger slipping into her at just the right moment, and her wave of sweet, ashamed, and grateful pleasure.

How indelible is your mark, Earl?

Those hands, the first on her in that way, that mouth, the first on her in that way. Turning her over and fucking her in that way. The first in that way.

Feeling no humiliation, or at least not that she was aware of. Nor degradation. Not for years and years.

In the photos his little pig eyes stare out at her from his stocky fatness. She can hear his voice. Get over here. I got something for you.

There may be no sex or intimacy in her life any more, but there is no violence, either. She is safe. Her house is predictable and warm, and its security system ensures that no one gets in. When she is out in the world no one gets in, either – the Liz Claiborne clothes, the hundred-dollar haircut, the two-hundred-dollar shoes, the hard look of complete confidence – she has fooled the world, with her clothes and with her air of cool, quiet control. And she had almost fooled herself, until today. This moment. When she compares herself to Elsa again. Elsa is as authentic as ever – the designer clothes look as natural on her today as the buckskin and beads did in the Valley.

Rose feels so guilty she is almost dizzy. She abandoned Elsa when Elsa had finally needed *her* for a change. She should have been there for her, and she wasn't. She had chickened out, hadn't even called. In the face of danger, any danger, the best she has ever done is run away. She has never acted courageously, has never helped save anyone. She is a coward. And now here is Elsa, almost directly in front of her, and if Elsa turns her head slightly, maybe Rose will see the scar. And she doesn't want to.

Elsa disappears from the mirror, and for a terrifying split second she is real, close enough for Rose to speak to. Frozen with fear, Rose holds her breath. And then Elsa, brave Elsa, beautiful even with the pale scar across her cheek, is gone again, taking the past with her, vanished into a change room, and Rose is alone, and safe, again.

her heart's *content*

*M*auve tipped the kitchen stool against the refrigerator. She opened the freezer compartment door and got herself an Aero bar. Then she tipped her stool back onto its four legs. She placed the chocolate bar on the counter in front of her, unwrapped it slowly, and watched as the old girl came out of the house across the street. She watched her descend the three steps. Solid concrete, those steps, and relatively new; put in last summer. Must have had a small windfall from someplace, Mauve thought at the time. When the big truck came and dumped the precast steps on the sidewalk, and the men manoeuvred them into place below the metal front door. Now she wondered if it was done for the old guy. Mauve broke the chocolate bar into pieces and lined them up horizontally in front of her, like cards for solitaire. She ate the pieces slowly, left to right.

The old guy used to come out the door ahead of his wife, but much slower, if that could be imagined. And when they walked together, they didn't walk together. He walked ahead as they made their way around the block. Moving like a couple of unfriendly snails. Man and wife.

Last Monday morning around eleven the ambulance pulled up across the street. Complete with entourage – police, fire engine, hangers-on. Wahoo, Wahoo. Bells and sirens. Mauve ate her chocolate bars and watched the paramedics run in and out of the house. They bundled the old guy up and took him out to the ambulance. Mauve watched the old girl come out after him, make her way down the stairs, and laboriously climb into the back of the vehicle. No one helped her. No one ever helped her. The old girl's face revealed nothing; it was as blank as always. Her hair looked uncombed, slept on. She wore a black ski jacket and grey pants, and scuffed, black, slip-on boots. Anything could be read on that face. So the old girl went off in the ambulance with her husband. And the next day, Tuesday, and every day since, she walked around the block alone. In her black ski jacket. Her scuffed, black boots. A scarf tied carelessly and tightly around her frizzy grey hair. Mauve tried to read her body for clues as to whether the old guy had lived or not, but she could tell nothing. There was no special unsteadiness in her walk; there was nothing readable on her face; there was no greater stoop in her shoulders. Or not that Mauve could detect.

Maybe he had been absent for years, she decided, and so the step over into death was a small one. Maybe he required so much care he exhausted his poor, simple wife and she was more exhausted than stunned. Maybe he was a son of a bitch and drank. It was hard to say. Mauve had never said two words to him, had never been within ten yards of him.

She reached into the freezer again, for a KitKat this time. She broke the fingers apart and made them into a square, then a "U," and then an "L," and finally an "I," as she munched them slowly, one at a time. Her stomach growled. It must be close to lunchtime. Rex would be home soon. She set the timer for four minutes. Her son Michael's favourite number when he was small. And then she ate the last finger, and there was nothing in front of her on the counter but empty space, into which she put her hands.

A truck pulled up across the street. One of the woman's daughters, come to fetch her laundry or her kids or both. Today it was the skinny blonde with the tight jeans. Driving the blue Ford that needs a muffler. She kept her cigarette in her mouth and smoked it right up to the bottom of the steps and then she threw it towards the street. It rolled down the sidewalk. All three of the kids, all tough-looking daughters, do this. The old guy must be, or must have been, on oxygen. The young woman went into the house. Came back out again two minutes later dragging an eight-year-old girl in a grubby pink ski jacket. No laundry. Either it wasn't dry or there wasn't any today. Mauve peered at the woman until she turned to light her next cigarette. She glanced up and Mauve could see her raw, red eyes. Her face looked broken. He must have died. Then the truck pulled away.

A minute later the door opened again and the old girl stepped out. This morning she glanced up when she went down the steps. Almost caught Mauve's eye, but not quite. Then the timer went off.

She had better get dressed before she hears Rex whistling his happy tune on his way home for lunch. He whistled more than he spoke now – modern upbeat hymns they sang regularly at his church.

Does all that God stuff help, Rex? she asked him once. Does it really help?

The Lord in His mercy tries, Mauve, he answered.

You have no idea how false that sounds, Rex, she told him.

It works for me, Mauve. That's the main thing, wouldn't you say? He looked her in the eye. What works for you?

Nothing, she replied. Nothing works for me.

Once she could hear Rex down the street it was certain he would catch her like this, and he didn't like her to be in her nightclothes at noon. She couldn't imagine why. She stretched out a leg. Her big toes had almost pushed their way through her slip-on terry cloth slippers. She shrugged and sighed and pulled at a curl on her forehead. She hopped without grace off the stool. Crunched the foil and paper chocolate bar wrappers into a tight hard ball and opened the garbage can lid. Lifted a milk container and a TV dinner tray and tucked the wrappers underneath. Closed the lid. Tipped the last of the now very strong tea into her pink china mug and took it with her down the hall. In the foyer, she poured the cold tea into a spider plant.

Last night she dreamed she was nursing Michael, and he drank happily, and eagerly. He smiled up at her with his crinkly brown eyes. This is love, she thought. This is it: the pureness could kill you. Like heroin. Light you up like a Christmas tree. Then she rocked him, her sated and sleepy porkball of a baby smiling drunkenly against her chest. His mouth ringed with milk. The tiny starfish hand splayed against her breast, milk still dripping from the elongated nipple. Mauve lowered her head to the top of his and kissed his hair, his warm skull. I can smell you, Mauve whispered, and started to cry.

It had almost killed her to wake up, to face the truth. She lay in bed on her back, her slack breasts falling each to one side against her upper arms. Her breathing was short, shallow. She wished she would die.

At first she couldn't speak. Clenched the sheets in her fists, jaw tight, words a thousand miles from her tongue.

Mauve? Are you still in bed?

No, she said softly.

MAUVE!

She forced herself to a sitting position. Out in a minute, she called.

She sat with her head in her hands. This was too hard today. Every day was too hard. Every month, every year was too hard. It was a lie to say it got easier. So difficult to choose what to wear, because it didn't matter. It didn't matter and so she could only turn her head and stare at the skirts and blouses hanging in her closet, at the colourful sweatshirts on the shelf, the rows of squared scarves and rolled belts. Rex kept things tidy and organized around here. He wears his shirts two days before tossing them into the dry cleaner's hamper. After the first day he takes off his tie, then his shirt. He hangs it back up on its hanger and does up the first button to keep it hanging straight. He keeps his jackets and pants under the dry cleaner's plastic even after he's worn them more than once. Rustles the plastic down over them when he hangs them back up at night before bed. Before he sits on the edge of the bed with his eyes closed, his hands folded in his lap, saying his prayers. What do you pray for, Rex? she wonders. He seems so perfectly fine, so perfectly self-contained. Beyond, or above, feeling. Rex vacuumed, Rex shopped, Rex cleaned the bathroom. And she? She?

She had to get dressed. It was worse if she didn't get dressed. She might not move for days. And Rex –

Hey Mauve! Do you think a fellow could get some lunch?

Yes. I'm coming. She dropped her housecoat on the bedroom floor. She lifted her flannel nightie up over her head and tossed it onto the pile of laundry beside the hamper. She reached into the pile of laundry and pulled out pink sweatpants. She buttoned up a dark blue cardigan.

Laundry day, she said as she came into the kitchen. Not much to wear.

I don't have to come home, you know. I don't have to interrupt your busy schedule.

I know. I'm sorry.

Rex looked snazzy, even with the frown. Not a hint

of tragedy about him. There never was. He had one hand on his hip under his sports jacket, one hand shaking his bunch of keys. Dignified grey at his temples. Mr. Salesman. Mr. *Christian* Salesman. A small New Testament in his breast pocket. Every morning Rex shined his shoes. Every day he washed his hair. Every day he wore clean shorts, and socks. Every day he sat on a dining-room chair in good light and picked lint off his jacket before he left the house for work. Every day he went out and entered the world.

I like it that you come home for lunch, she said. Sit down.

That's my girl, said Rex. Now we're talking. Just give me a minute to change my tie – the seam's come open on this one.

She tied on an apron, got out a tall glass and put in two ice cubes. She filled the glass with tomato juice. Got the Worcestershire sauce out of the fridge. Handed him a teaspoon. When she refilled the ice cube tray she spilled water on the counter and swept it off onto the floor with her forearm. Rex didn't notice. He opened a section of the paper, folded it, then folded it again. New ads aren't in yet, he said. Boss is ticked right off. Mauve lifted the grilled cheese sandwich out of the frying pan and slipped it onto a plate. Slipped it off again to cut it into four on the counter. Michael's favourite number. Mauve watched Rex as he ate, drank, read. She inspected her nails. Picked some of the pills off her pants.

You know, if you didn't come home for lunch, I might *never* get dressed, she said.

What's that? said Rex, looking up.

I think the old guy died, Mauve said.

What old guy?

The one across the street.

Oh, him.

She walks by herself now. I saw her again today. In her black ski jacket. I told you before about the ambulance.

Did you?

Yes. The other day. Last week.

Well, he looked like hell the last time I saw him, whenever that was.

The girls have been coming around. The daughters. I've seen the red Camaro, the black pickup truck, the blue pickup truck.

Is that right.

And one day soon they'll all show up wearing dresses and suits, and they will all look awkward in them. For the funeral. Rex?

Mm?

No one ever walks with the mum. She's always alone, sort of drifting along.

Is that right. Thanks for lunch, he said. That was good.

You're welcome.

Mauve, your sister Carmine called again last night. You should call her.

Stop saying that.

Call your sister, Mauve.

No.

It was an accident, Mauve. A long time ago now. It was an accident.

Just leave me alone, Rex, she said, feeling the anger rise in her. Just bugger off, would you? And then she was off the stool and pushing him out the door, her anger propelling her, pushing, pushing his reluctant bulk. *Go, I said. Get out of here. GO! GO!*

You go, said Rex. *You* get off that self-pitying ass of yours and get to the phone and talk to your sister.

Then he paused.

Mauve? Listen to me. I've been thinking. There's these new condos down by the river.

She looked at him.

And?

I was just thinking. Maybe we should move.

Move?

Move on. You know. Bill and Carmine got a new place. Bill says it's great.

I can't move.

I'd help you.

You and *God,* I suppose. You just don't get it, do you Rex? *You* don't feel anything. You never have, have you? Mauve felt memory and pain flood through her. *You* listen to *me,* Rex: *I* felt his fingers hold onto my finger, as he and I walked down the street together. This street, the one right here. You know what he said to me, Rex? He said, I am so happy that I love you! That's what he said to me. On our sidewalk. Right here, Rex. He climbed that lilac. He tipped over on his tricycle, over there. He stepped down these steps and trotted over to the car. Here. There. Right where you're standing. You don't feel anything, do you? Do you? Rex stepped back, turned away. Then he said, Sit on that stool forever, then. Sit there to your heart's content,

Mauve. But he's still dead. We laid him out, we buried him in that little grey suit, and he's *gone.* You've got to stop it, Mauve. You're driving me crazy, too. Do you hear me?

Mauve had put her hands against her ears as soon as she heard the word "dead." She hummed loudly, so that the hum in her head drowned out his voice. And so she didn't hear him cry. She didn't see him cry. When she opened her eyes he was gone.

Dead. Except to you, is what he had said as he wept. You carry him around *in*side you like you used to carry him around *out*side you. It hurts to watch it. It hurts too much. You hear me, Mauve? Ah, fuck it.

Mauve examined her face in the side of the toaster. The sore place on her jawline was gone, though there was a small round scar. It had started out as a pimple, but she worried and pestered it into more. Then she kept picking off the scab, so it never quite healed. After a while a little mound of scar tissue grew there, which she snipped off one day with small sharp scissors. That hurt. As it began to heal, she picked at the rough edges. She grimaced and held her breath as she pulled off the tough scab. She grew peculiarly fond of this small, bothered wound even as she knew she must, really must, leave it be. She promised herself not to touch it, allowed herself only to run her fingers along the uneven surface when she found it slightly healed in the morning. But before long, her fingernails had begun a slow and painful tugging, tugging. She liked that it hurt. The pain grew familiar.

Back in the bedroom she unbuttoned her cardigan all the way down. With her left hand she held her right breast. Held the left breast with the right hand. How slack and worthless they were now. The two of them. But there was a time. When Rex's hand on her nipple alone could bring her to orgasm. Sex had always been good. *Let's make us a baby, Mauvie. Just one? How about twenty? she teased.* Especially during the pregnancy. She was lusty the whole time she carried Michael. Now she gently tweaked her nipples. Nothing. That too was dead.

She lay down and curled up on the bed.

Michael. Only she knew the taste of him between his toes, the scent of him behind his ears. Only she had ever kissed every square inch of him, every round, soft inch of him from head to precious foot. There was nothing like him. Inside and out. At Christmastime she knew God's joy at having a son. She figured she was God and all the angels combined. She sang. *Unto us a son is given.* She knew awe: love and fear. The looks of love they exchanged took away her breath. He seduced her completely, he brought her great joy. Her boy, her love, her boy. She ached to kiss him again. Once. Just once.

That last spring every animal, person, or invention he drew had to have a yellow nose. Every morning he wanted porridge with brown sugar and milk. Every day he rode his tricycle. She strode quickly to keep up. You must stop at the corners and wait for me because you have to be safe, she said. I will be safe, Mummy, he said, promising. I will be safe.

And now he was gone.

Michael had been visiting his cousins for the weekend. Mauve didn't want him to go; he had never been away from home overnight. But everyone begged her to let him, and finally she relented. She and Rex drove him to Carmine and Bill's big subdivision house together and left him. Carmine in her silk caftans, standing on the steps of that pink monstrosity of a house. Michael called it a castle. He was so excited he didn't want to say goodbye, he only had eyes for his cousins, Troy and Cal.

The next day, Mauve's sister Carmine was on the phone when Michael slid open her unlatched patio door and slipped out. Carmine was ordering sleeping bags from Sears. Her two boys were watching a video, and she thought Michael was with them. Michael padded across the wooden deck in his bare feet, went down the stairs, walked over to the edge of the pool and reached out for the blow-up tiger that was floating near the edge.

Where is Michael? Carmine asked her sons when she got off the phone. Where is your cousin?

Be quiet, Mum, said the one. I can't hear.

Where is your cousin?

Don't know, said the other. He didn't like the scary part, so he went away.

Unto us a Child is born...
Unto us a Son is given...

It was Bill who jumped in and lifted him out. Who laid him at the side of the pool. Who called 911. Who called them. Rex answered the phone.

She has seen her sister once since it happened, at the funeral, though she wouldn't talk to her. For a long time Carmine wrote, Carmine called, invited Mauve to come and visit.

Blame?

Accidents happen.

Blame?

Yes.

Mauve and Rex looked at each other with wild, stricken eyes. Never, ever again would they see each other so raw, and honest. Skinned and gutted alive in less than a minute. *Everything* fell out, wet and hot. Guts. Heart.

She had shopped for Michael, as she always had. A small grey suit, dove grey, a white shirt with a fine blue line. In the Eaton's boys' department. Socks. Underwear. Suit. Tie. All brand new: he would have liked that. How old is he? asked the clerk. Three and a half, she said. She shined his small black shoes.

She doesn't hate Carmine, though sometimes she wonders why. But in the end it makes no difference. There is a soft, grey nothingness where her feelings used to be. Anger the only one she can ever muster. Otherwise, her interior is a shapeless, formless place that offers no resistance, nor any hot or cold, warmth or coolness, to the touch of thought. Empty and undefined. Filling her entirely sometimes. This grey fog.

Mauve opened a KitKat. She made an "M" and ate it.

The old girl's house used to be stucco. Stucco with the sparkle gone or too dirty to see. Beige trim worn off the windowsills. Rotting steps, swaybacked and sloped. One day last summer a big truck drove up. Great sugar tongs lifted the concrete steps down off the back of the truck and onto the sidewalk. Then the old steps were gone and the new ones were in place. Just like that. A day later the wrought iron railings were added. The white vinyl siding took another day and a half. They didn't do the sides of the house, just the front, and the back of the garage.

What, she wondered, had the old guy died of? A heart attack? Maybe not his first. Then the walks were to strengthen him, get the blood moving, the heart pumping. Around the block was the better part of an hour. He never got any better. He was doomed.

Could she, she wondered, could she get off her "self-pitying ass" and mend Rex's tie for him? She could try. It wouldn't take much. She could sit right here and do it.

The tie is folded neatly on Rex's dresser. He is ridiculously tidy. He keeps his shoes shaped with shoe trees, and the pairs of shoes are divided into work and leisure on the closet floor. His shirts and his belt rack are organized according to colour. Something catches her eye. It's Michael's cowboy belt, hanging with Rex's. She fingers it. Then in Rex's dresser drawers she finds more of Michael's things. Rocks. Hard lumps of PlayDoh. A handful of Duplo. Little underwear folded alongside

Rex's underwear. Small socks rolled up amongst his rolled-up socks. Mauve stands staring, builds and unbuilds the pieces of Duplo. And then she starts to cry. She hadn't known. How could she have known? He has said nothing, because there has been nothing to say. Rex has said nothing.

She waits. In the stillness of the house, Mauve sits waiting on the floor outside Michael's bedroom door. The furnace is off. Not a fan, not a tick, not a sound. She ought to be able to hear his breathing behind the door. The house is so still she can feel her own heart, feel the pulse of her body. The cup of her right hand rests against her ear. She listens. Kathumpathumpathumpa. Her heart. Sends the blood coursing round and round. Keeps her alive. Keeps him alive.

At four she gets up off the floor, and opens the door. The afternoon sun pours in the windows; the curtains are gone. Only the tracks and the cord remain, naked, ugly. The room is empty; everything is gone. Dents in the lino where the bed and dresser stood. His desk. All his clothes and shoes from the closet, all his puzzles, his Lego, his toys. Everything, everything is gone. The naked light switch is ugly and bare. The light bulb in the centre of the ceiling is ugly and bare. There's a dead bee on the floor. No point even saying Michael's name. He is gone.

It has been a while since Mauve wore a dress, and it feels rather nice, actually. To stand in front of the mirror in her slip, brushing her hair. To see her legs in stockings, feel the silky brushing against each other and her slip. She likes the shift in how she carries herself when she puts on heels instead of slippers, and how the heels make her hips swing as she walks. Not bothering to undo all the buttons up the front, she slips a green wool dress over her head. And when she perches herself on the kitchen stool, she feels a little bit sexy as she unbuttons the top and bottom buttons of her dress.

Across the street, she can see the cars and trucks arrive one by one. The daughters and their families climb out. The daughters smoke their cigarettes until they reach the bottom of the steps, then throw the butts towards the street. Exhale the last of the smoke as they all go in the house together. They look awkward in their dress clothes, their skirts and heels, their suits and dress shoes. A short while later, they all come out again. Last to emerge is the old girl, in a grey suit, black shoes, and carrying a black purse. She has a new hairdo. A perm, soft and curly. She makes her way down the steps alone, and she looks up, not down, as she descends. She looks like a million bucks. The back door of one of the cars opens and in she climbs.

Death can make a new woman of you, thinks Mauve, so mesmerized by the scene that, when the phone rings, she answers.

quick*sand*

*t*he complex was designed with a central courtyard containing rhododendrons and tulip trees and benches placed so that residents and their guests can sit and watch birds at the feeders. Inside the building, a black lab or a cat might accompany you partway down the hall before it turns and pads quietly into someone's room to visit. You pass animal cages – hamster, chinchilla, rabbits, budgies – and you pass signs posted on the walls about the residents' rights, and notices encouraging people to get involved with the politics and pastimes of the place. There is a large chapel containing two pianos, one upright, one grand, as well as an organ. At the end of this room, behind a tall accordion sliding door, are a giant TV, and some comfortable chairs. There is a sunny arts and crafts room, and there are several pleasant lounge areas. And the attitude presented by the nurses, orderlies, and other employees feels genuinely caring and helpful.

No matter what, however, you can never quite forget that this is a kind of hospital. The smells, the colours, are hospital smells and colours. This is a place of transition, a place that will lead inevitably to death for all the people who live here, though it takes some much longer than others to find their way there. Walking towards Aunt May's room I pass photographs of people who turned one hundred during their stay. What they have in common is that they look spry, and happy, if ancient. In some of the pictures the people pose with the animals – a woman in a wheelchair holds a rabbit on her lap; her gnarled hand rests quietly on its soft, furry back. Another woman gently pats the head of a golden retriever. A man smiles as he feeds crackers to a white cockatoo. Contact. That's what it's about, I think as I approach Aunt May's door. Contact of all kinds, but never ever *no* physical contact, *no* touch. We stroke an animal, kiss our child. The saddest part of growing old might be that you will never again be touched by someone fond of you, if they are all gone, or all dead, or all too far away and absorbed in their own lives. Or if they are too afraid of your condition – your sickness, your age – to touch you. And that you yourself will have no one to touch, no one who wants you to touch them.

The men and women pictured on these walls are not the ones moaning "Help Me! Help Me!" as I walk past. They are not the ones who sit passively, heads bowed low against their chests as they wait for nothing or anything. No, they are more like the woman all dolled up with rouge, pink lipstick, and yellow chiffon head scarf, briskly pushing her walker and her oxygen down the hall. A fluorescent green sticker on the oxygen tank reads, "Smile! It won't kill you!" She smiles at me brightly. And they are more like the man at the front entrance, who greets everyone, "Hello there! Good Morning! Lovely Day!" There must be something in these people before they get here, something that enables them to be happy wherever they are. Something in their life that has prepared them for any circumstance or eventuality. What is it? I want to get some, before I, too, get old. I, who have inherited such a penchant for unhappiness and discontent.

Aunt May is alone in her room when I go in; she is stooped over in her wheelchair with her back to the window. The curtains are partly drawn. Rachmaninoff is playing on a portable stereo. Aunt May doesn't hear, or doesn't care, when I enter. I crouch down beside her and I speak very softly.

Hello, Aunt May. It's Ann. She lifts her head a little. How are you, Aunt May?

Oh Ann. Hello dear. I'm fine, I guess, she says meekly, and her eyes rise barely enough to meet mine, then fall again.

My sisters are here too, Aunt May. They'll be here in a minute. We thought we'd start with just one of us.

I kiss her soft, soft cheek. Pull a chair up close to her, sit, and take her hand in mine. I am so glad to see you, I say, and it's true. She has always been so warm and gentle; so calm, and reasonable. Everything her sister, our mother, is not.

The multiple sclerosis first made itself known when Aunt May was in her forties. She was golfing when she noticed something odd: her foot went to sleep, and didn't wake up. The numbness didn't change, and it didn't go away. Gradually, the area it affected got bigger. She became clumsier, started dropping dishes and glasses, miscalculating steps, bumping into things. Driving one day she found herself unable to lift her foot off the gas, and she had an accident. The disease's advancement was very, very slow, overall, took years and years and years to get to where it is now. Slower than molasses, she replied when I asked her how long. As slow as can be imagined.

Her house, all on one level, was bought while the disease was still in its early stages. In anticipation of the inevitable future, the doorways were enlarged to allow wheelchair access; there are bars in the bathroom; utensils and dishes are within reaching distance from a wheelchair. From her living room Aunt May could see the garden, see the roses around the patio through her plate glass patio doors. Plenty of roses: she was born in May.

She woke up one Sunday a month ago paralyzed from the neck down. She waited in her bed (I almost add "patiently" but how else, when you are paralyzed like that, could you wait, I wonder?) for her friend Cora to come in her light blue Mercedes to take her to church. It was Cora who called the ambulance.

The doctors who examined and evaluated Aunt May told her that although she would regain some feeling in her hands and arms and neck, she could never go home again. She would have to sell her house, save the money for her care.

It must seem to her as though she has moved into the West Edmonton Mall at Christmastime. So many people here, all strangers. So much coming and going. All of it unfamiliar. For the past twenty years the MS had pretty well confined her to home. Uncle Mac died of a heart attack ten years ago, and she has been alone most of the time since then. Has been accustomed to spending her days quietly, with her black fluffball of a cat, Susie, sitting on her lap purring deeply. The only surprise in her day might be the telephone's occasional and welcome ring, or a delivery person at the front door bringing mail orders. A benign existence while the less than benign disease slowly, slowly ravaged her.

Aunt May and Uncle Mac had no children, and no close relatives except for her sister. And so Aunt May asked us, Pearl's four daughters, Marnie, Laurel, Roberta, and Ann, to go there, to go to her house in Tacoma. She wanted us, she said, to take what we liked, to divide it all up, and arrange to dispose of the rest. And then to sell the house.

On a weekend in May we go. From Campbell River, from Enderby, from Vancouver, from Saskatoon. The four sisters, 52, 45, 39, 38, who have not spent more than three hours in each other's company alone for dozens of years. Never without kids around. Never overnight. And certainly never on a mission like this.

Marnie gets the house key from the neighbour across the street and we enter Aunt May's house. It feels strange to be here when she is not. The house is still. It smells strongly of cat urine, but we see no cat; the pet door onto the patio is open.

In the foyer Laurel begins to cry. (She always begins to cry.) Stands there like a fourteen-year-old. It's so sad, she sobs. I feel so awful. I feel so sad for her. Automatically we take her in our arms. Oh Laurel. Don't cry.

We dump our luggage, call for the cat, who does not come. Marnie cuts some roses from the garden, we get back in the cars and go to see Aunt May.

It's so very nice to see you all, Aunt May says softly.

Is there anything you'd like us to bring you from your house, Aunt May?

I can't think of anything, dear. But thank you for the roses.

How about Susie? Would you like us to bring Susie to see you?

I don't think so. I think it might be too sad for me.

Aunt May? says Laurel. I'd really like to adopt Susie. I was wondering – would that be all right with you?

Aunt May brightens a little, lifts her head. I've been worrying about what would happen to Susie.

I'd really like to have a kitty.

You could take her home with you. She can become a Canadian cat.

I'd like to do that, Aunt May. I'd like to do that very much.

There is light in Aunt May's eyes by the time we leave that first day. It makes us feel good. All our lives we have been told we are a nuisance, are in the way, are selfish and thoughtless, and Aunt May's pleasure at our presence helps us all. On the way back to her house we stop at a liquor store and a takeout cappuccino stand.

We stop at Fred Meyer's so Laurel can buy a harness and a leash for Susie.

Because our methods of working are so different, we decide that to avoid conflict, each of us will take a room. Laurel attacks the kitchen. Empties the cupboards onto the counter and then sorts through the contents. When a cupboard is empty, she puts a piece of orange tape on it so we know not to bother opening the door: there is nothing inside. She is like a cyclone.

Roberta can't get started; she has to think, she says. She feels she is violating Aunt May, she says, even though Aunt May has asked us to do this. Feels it is wrong to open her private drawers, go through her things and then take them. She pulls out her cigarettes and goes out on the patio.

Marnie kneels in the spare bedroom, surrounded by old photo albums, records, reel-to-reel tapes, boxes of slides. She is steady, competent, focused. Look at this, you guys! each of us calls from time to time. Come and see this!

I head to the master bedroom. Two single beds pushed together, a bedside table and a dresser on each side. The top drawer of her dresser is filled with underwear; the second contains scarves, all ironed and folded neatly; the third contains gifts from our mother. A glasses case from Mexico. A silver-clad perfume bottle from Costa Rica. A silk scarf from Japan. Small things that are easily mailed from the exotic locales our mother has liked to frequent.

In Uncle Mac's dresser there are no undershorts or socks, but there are dozens of monogrammed handkerchiefs, a generous selection of cufflinks and tie pins, three gold watches with fobs, a camera, and a light meter. In the walk-in closet, all his shirts, suits, pants and shoes are gone, but his plaid wool dressing gown hangs close beside Aunt May's.

In the ensuite is a toilet with a high plastic seat so Aunt May could move from her wheelchair onto the toilet. A big package of incontinence pads stands in one corner. The bathroom drawers are filled, along with medicine and first aid items, with pretty soaps people have given her, and with every colour of lipstick imaginable, purchased by mail order.

We push the furniture in the living room to one side to make room for the various piles: things the person sorting believes that none of us will want; things one or more of us might possibly want; things someone will certainly want. This works well. We've parked Aunt May's red electric scooter beside the grand piano; we'll take it home to our mother. The piano will be given to the university where Uncle Mac taught. It was a wedding gift to our grandmother from our grandfather, though he could never bear to hear her play. The university people will pick it up next week, along with whatever music we don't want to keep.

Roberta crouches down between the piano and the music cabinet; there are stacks of sheet music in the bench and beside the piano legs as well. How important music was in their lives! She finds giant records tucked in behind the cabinet, records far too big for any player we can imagine. They contain symphonies Uncle Mac conducted in New York for radio broadcast. Roberta finds a hymn written by Uncle Mac, sits down at the piano and sight reads. And she finds a copy of *The Fireside Book of Folk Songs*. This book is as familiar to us as a family Bible is to others. We all know most of the songs, have been brought up singing them.

Saturday afternoon I need a break. I strip off my jeans and T-shirt, put on my running gear. I slip out the front door and I run. Hard. Around the neighbourhood. Over to the golf course. Up near the university. I run until I'm sweating buckets, and feel much better – a lot of tension is gone.

While I'm away, the house is still and quiet. Laurel is alone, going through books. Roberta and Marnie go out to buy garbage bags and round up more boxes. Susie comes cautiously through the cat door. Laurel coaxes her onto her knee and strokes her, speaks softly to her. Then she manages to slip on the harness and the leash. Susie tenses with suspicion. The harness is on but not buckled when I come suddenly through the front door after my run. My entrance spooks Susie; she takes off like a shot, out through the kitty door, trailing all the gear.

Ann! You idiot! I was just getting it on!

I'm sorry.

Damn it! She's gone.

I'm sorry. We'll find her. Don't worry.

But we don't. And in another hour the rain begins – thick, heavy rain.

The original intent was that we would sit down together for meals. Clear a space on the dining-room table and set it. Talk, release, discuss. But this never actually happens. One or more of us is always engaged in some project she doesn't want to leave. So each of us stands to eat, grabs a bite here, a bite there. A handful of spoons and knives are tossed onto the table. A tub of margarine and some ketchup. We eat familiar, simple things. Porridge. Tuna casserole. Grilled cheese sandwiches and tomato soup.

After supper Laurel goes out in the rain, and she finds the cat. Susie is next door, under a deck the size of a playing field and built close to the ground. Susie's pitiful meowing comes from somewhere near the middle. Laurel rings the doorbell, but the people are out. The rain continues to pour, and Susie continues to cry. We are all out in the rain now, coaxing the cat. We sweet-talk. We try to prod her with a branch. We poke at her with a rake handle. She does not budge. She will not or cannot come out. There is nothing more to be done. We're soaked and muddy from lying on our bellies. We go back to the house. That night Laurel can't sleep. Susie, her bequest, her responsibility, is starving, and soaking, trapped under the deck forever. But in the middle of the night Susie comes home, trailing the gear, and curls up on Laurel's chest.

In a steamer trunk in the garage we find Hudson's Bay wool blankets. Two engraved silver compacts, one of them a gift to Aunt May from our parents in 1942.

Sugar cubes from a hotel in Vienna. Fancy hotel soaps from a London hotel. Wool badges and a gold Head Girl's pin from the boarding school Aunt May attended in the 30s, St. Hilda's, in Calgary. And a blue taffeta evening dress. I shuck my clothes on the cement floor. I slip on the dress; it fits me. I love the swish of the skirt. The peaked bust; the strapless gown that billows out around mid-calf. The length of matching material that dignifies the dress, tucks in around the neck and down in front of each partially bared, now obscured breast. I go to the bedroom and add crystal earrings and necklace from Aunt May's jewellery box. I pin up my hair with hairpins. I pretend I am my aunt when she was a young woman, prance barefoot through the house.

We found a dress out in your garage, Aunt May, I tell her the next day. A beautiful blue dress, made of taffeta.

That was my wedding dress, she says. I married your Uncle Mac in that dress.

By Sunday noon, stress is etched on all our faces. We feel as though we have been struggling against drowning in all Aunt May's stuff. There is *so much*. Laurel says she feels like she's drunk eighty-nine cups of coffee. Marnie looks ripe for a migraine. Roberta chain-smokes. I have chewed off all my nails. A masseuse would find a million walnuts in our backs and shoulders. We have hugged each other often, and hard. We have ravaged and pillaged Aunt May's house utterly. And somehow, we have not fought.

Phillip and I live modestly in Saskatoon. Our small house has rough old floors and ancient, stained wallpaper. Into this house I will bring Aunt May's sterling silver flatware and candlesticks. Austrian and German china. White linen tablecloths and serviettes. Her wedding dress, her silver compact with the engraved "M." Trappings of a way of life that will never be mine. My portion of a life that has, in a sense, been drawn and quartered.

I take Phillip my uncle's wool greatcoat, and a gold toothpick in a brown leather case. I take him a white silk scarf that has never been out of its package. A gold pocket watch with a bloodstone in the fob. Breakable things are wrapped in towels and embroidered linens, doilies and sheets.

All that is left to do is return the house key to the neighbour. He will put out the garbage, and be there when the Salvation Army comes. Then we will visit Aunt May one more time. Perhaps, we know, for the very last time. We are heartsick, sad, and exhausted.

We take *The Fireside Book of Folk Songs* with us. We wheel Aunt May out of her room, down the hall, and into the chapel, situate her near the upright piano. I sit on one side, Laurel and Marnie on the other. Roberta plays. Aunt May sits quietly, listening to us sing. She herself doesn't, though we know she once had a fine voice. We sing "Skye Boat Song." We sing "Bendemeer's Stream." And then, during "Loch Lomond," Aunt May starts to sing. Her neck muscles aren't strong enough to keep her head up for long, and her head droops like a sunflower against her chest, but a wavering sweetness comes softly from her mouth. *You'll take the high road and I'll take the low road.... Me and my true love will never meet again.*

Her voice grows stronger in "The Blue Bells of Scotland." My sisters and I stop singing and listen to our aunt's sweet solo voice. *Suppose and suppose that your highland lad should die....* My throat closes, my eyes well up. How she must miss our uncle. How alone she must sometimes feel. What can one hope for in a place like this, with a disease like this? I stand and walk to the back of the chapel so that no one can hear me cry.

Aunt May told me once about a recurring nightmare she had until she was in her thirties. *I am walking along,* she said, *and I see something large and dark sinking in quicksand, and I am afraid it is going to happen to me. I am going to sink in the quicksand and be unable to get out. The quicksand is like a whirlpool of batter, very much like batter, going around and around and down.* I think hard about her heavy, failing body, the body that daily, slowly, sucks her spirit down.

Then I glance at Aunt May. *She* isn't crying – there is *life* in her eyes. And the sunflower of her head no longer rests loose against her chest; it is lifted.

the dog *next* door

i have just finished taking the wet garbage out to the compost. It is Thursday morning, you see, and I have had my breakfast cantaloupe, and the skin takes up rather a lot of room in the bucket. I do it again on Sunday, after my grapefruit. Having a regimen adds structure to my days, I find. And meaning: there is always something which must be done next. This is my comfort, since Malcolm died. You can ask me, Do I miss him? and I'll tell you: I cope.

On the way back from the compost I can hear that the three little boys next door have a new puppy. The first one, I recall, ran away some time ago. The second died of mysterious causes. Could have had to do with their dragging it around the yard by the neck, if you ask me. This third, I suspect, is from the SPCA. We'll see how long it lasts. I am not optimistic.

It's chilly out today; I'll have to remember to wear a

sweater when I go to get my hair done. Every Thursday without fail I take a taxi to that numbskull Shawna and wonder if this time she'll get my hair right at the sides, and every Thursday I come home twenty dollars and a dollar tip short, and unhappy with the sides. But what on earth else can I do? Go around like some frump of a cleaning woman? Give up and say, who cares what I look like, and sit down in a corner and die? Move to Chilliwack where my usual girl, Louise, ran off to? Not likely. So I'm at Shawna's mercy, and most weeks she's without that particular quality.

Doesn't life become complicated sometimes. I never had this problem with my hair when Malcolm was still here. Now, I know that doesn't make sense. I mean simply that somehow things have become harder, even things he had nothing directly to do with. Oh, and I know full well Louise had a right to move, to get married, as much as she had the right to wear those hideous plastic shoes she used to wear that must have pinched her feet so terribly I couldn't bear to look at them and finally told her so. But why did it have to be *my* girl who took it into her head to marry and move away? Why couldn't it have been that Mrs. Androchuk's girl? An army of hairdressers couldn't make that woman look decent. If just desserts were ever served in this life. But they aren't. And there's no point dwelling on it. As I used to tell Malcolm on occasion.

My taxi's just about due now, and the driver gets annoyed if I keep him waiting too long, but I risk his wrath and look out my screen door again. It won't kill the driver to wait. I'm still trying to get a quick peek at the new canine – I was unsuccessful all morning. Yes. There it is. Looks a little like a boxer crossed with a tiger cat. Oh, if Malcolm were here, he would call it cute, I suppose, would get right out there to meet it. Through this very door, and down those very steps. I would stand here just like this and watch him pull on his big blue cardigan as he walked, and remind myself to remind him to wash his hands afterwards because he's bound to forget.

The dog is still small yet, about the size of a large cat, but with a good-sized yap-yap-yap coming out of it. Already filling their yard with excrement, too, I see. Disgusting filth. But think on the positive side, Bernice, I tell myself: maybe this dog will catch the one or two cats that miraculously escape Kujo's grip. Kujo, I should tell you, is the big mongrel in the yard on my other side. If I had a cat-killing dog on both sides, my garden might be completely unsullied. Imagine that! Now *that* would give me cause to rejoice, let me tell you. There is nothing worse than coming upon cat excrement when you're digging in the garden.

Unlike me, Malcolm was a dog person, a cat person, a mouse person, a you-name-it person. God's creatures. You'll find God in everything that lives and breathes, he'd say. Look into a dog's eyes, Bernice. You'll see the Divine in there. What about in this mosquito, Mal? I'd say. Look out, God! And then I'd smack it. Or I'd tease him with, I hope you cleared out of the cows, God; we're having hamburger tonight. Malcolm just smiled. Always smiling, that man, until he got sick. Too much of the patience of a saint in him, if you ask me. Didn't make him much of a fighter, now did it? And he damn well needed to be a fighter. If nothing else.

Where is that driver? I'm going to be late. In the yard the little boys wear gloves and the puppy leaps up to nip at them. The more they raise their hands, the more the puppy leaps. That'll teach it. The boys shriek and run and the puppy chases them. They tease it with a stick yanked out of its grip until its yelps of excitement turn into ones of frustration and anger. Stupid little boys can't tell the difference. Think it's all a game. Think life is all a game. Laughing, and laughing. Well, laugh while you can, fellows. Laugh while you can. You're in for a rude awakening one of these days, when life hits you square in the face.

The boys lose interest in their game, and climb up on the garage roof, where they play soldier and sabotage with the piled-up snow. Maybe they'll fall off and break their wretched little necks. The dog, below, looks as though its feelings have been hurt, the way it stands and watches them, nub of a tail wagging just a little. Too bad for you, too, puppy. Get used to it or perish. Feelings are a dime a dozen these days, and not much else costs so little anymore.

For heaven's sake. I haven't heard the taxi driver honking the horn and now he's at the door. I'll pay for this, rest assured, and it won't be the first or last time. You never get something for nothing in this world, especially not time.

When I get home from the hairdresser's, unhappy, as always, with my hair, the children next door have gone inside or away, and the puppy is entertaining himself by attempting to get into my yard. I watch him wriggle and flail as he tries to squeeze himself under the fence. How many times have I told their mother to get that fence fixed? Here he comes. Victory is his. He keeps out of my garden, anyway. Concentrates on the snowbank by the steps. Lucky for him. I make my tea, sit down with my Dad's cookies on a plate.

We never had a pet. I confess that I told Malcolm I was allergic, though I do wonder sometimes whether he believed me. Well, I was *mentally* allergic, for sure. That Malcolm. He would pat even the strays that walked down the sidewalk, calling them to him, scratching their ears and their behinds, worry about where their next meal was coming from. And then he'd forget to wash his hands. I'd have to get after him. Time and time again.

The next time I look out, the puppy has wriggled under my fence into the next yard. It is a good thing that Kujo is not out. He's a wily thing. Lies in wait for the cats in the dark, or under the porch, lies as still as a boulder on a beach. I'll be woken up or called from my cards by a sudden loud scuffle outside my bedroom window and yowls that make my blood run cold. I don't need to look out to know there's one less cat in the neighbourhood. Kujo's kitty kibble. Nature's way, now, isn't it? Prey on the unsuspecting.

A little while later the boys are knocking at my door. They are looking for their puppy, Benny. You have a new dog? I say, feigning innocence. (Quite a feat, at my age, I think, smiling inwardly.) No, I'm afraid I haven't seen him. I close the door. There's no point making their hunt any easier. Maybe they'll be a little less lackadaisical about looking after the dog if it takes them a while to locate him.

A few evenings later I see the boys' mother out in the yard, trying to block the hole under the fence. I'm not otherwise occupied, so I go out to chat. Why not? I feel sorry for that woman. She's certainly got both her hands full. She is one of these single mothers; she works long hours at the water treatment plant. And not a man in sight.

How's the puppy doing? I say.

It's nipping everyone, she says, resting her elbow on the fence and almost lying on it. She looks exhausted. I'm afraid it's going to bite someone.

Well your offspring are teaching it to do just that, I should have said. But I held my tongue. It's not my business, and what do I know about dogs but what any human being with even a scant one quarter of their brain working might know?

Maybe it needs to learn a different way of playing, I say.

Maybe, she says, not really hearing me. I don't know what to do.

Does it have a toy? A stick? A ball? It could play fetch.

Well, the boys had something out here. A tennis ball, I think. But I don't know where it's gone. She looks around helplessly.

Do you think the dog is getting enough exercise?

I try to get the boys to take him for a walk. I told them, if you took turns, it would be only every third day.

Or if you take him to the park, he could really run, I suggest.

But if he gets off his leash, he won't come back, says my neighbour.

Next day I see the youngest boy leave the house. He has the puppy on a leash. They go to the end of the block and back. Then he ties the dog to the porch and plays hockey by himself. The puppy yips and cries. SHUT UP! the boy yells. I have heard the tone before. It is how his older brothers yell at him. It's a darn good thing that Malcolm isn't here to witness this. He'd go pale with anger and rush right out there to give that child what for. Nicely, of course. Malcolm could always do things nicely. He had that way about him.

Sick of your puppy already? I say out the window.

No, he says, glaring at me. But it won't be quiet. And the boy goes into the house, leaving the dog to yip.

Oh, the nights can be long. I don't like the television, get annoyed with the radio announcers and their awful diction, even on the CBC, for goodness sake, so more often than not I sit in silence at my cards. I play until a quarter to ten, and then I go to bed. Each night, I confess, I run my cheek against the soft lamb's wool collar of Malcolm's sky blue sweater in bed beside me. Where he slept for all those years.

Thursday has rolled around once more, and my appointment's at one. The puppy next door has escaped from their yard again. One minute I could hear it whining, the next minute it was quiet. But I don't have time to watch out for it. That puppy will have to fend for itself. This time I hear the driver honk, and I'm ready. As I get in the cab, I think I hear some commotion around the back of my house. But then, it could be the driver's radio. He's got it on so loud I can't hear myself think. *I* certainly couldn't drive with such a noise in my ears. I close the car door and off we go.

Miracle of miracles, Shawna gets the sides close to right. I hope she's not fool enough to think I'll tip her more than my standard dollar, however. She'll have to prove it isn't just a fluke, and then I might reconsider. For next time. We'll see. Maybe there's hope for the girl after all. Taking the picture in may have helped. Like *this,* I said, as though I were talking to a small child. Do you think you could make my hair look like *this?* Oh, there's no love lost between Shawna and me. We just put up with each other, and both of us know it.

As soon as I get home, I go upstairs to the bathroom to check my hair. Oh happy day – my mirror reports the same thing as the beauty parlour's. I will celebrate by having my tea in one of mother's Limoges cups instead of my usual Royal Albert. But before I go down, I glance out my bedroom window.

There's that Kujo. He is on his side, sound asleep on the neighbour's wooden porch. Big, hulking, ugly thing that he is. How did God think up a creature like that? If Malcolm were here, I'd ask him, and he'd come up with some kind of an answer. Kujo's tongue looks soft and ruffled as a large pink lasagna noodle, still and wet between rows of enormous white teeth and black-lined dog lips.

Below the porch, on the soggy grass, lies the puppy. Or, rather, the puppy's body. His tiger fur is as saturated, his body as still, as the long brown grass under last year's rotting leaves.

Didn't I say? Didn't I?

I shake my head. I go downstairs and have my tea, though the celebration is spoiled by what I've had to see, and my hands are all atremble. And there's no relief during my nap. I dream that Kujo has that puppy in his jaws, is shaking it like a rabbit. Its neck is broken. The little head swings freely back and forth.

Stop that! Kujo! You stop that this instant! Malcolm yells, but Kujo doesn't hear a word he says, pays no attention whatsoever. Keeps on shaking that puppy until that puppy is good and dead.

It's not right, says Malcolm, white and shaken. To treat a creature like that. It's not right.

It's not right for you to have that cancer, either, I retort, furious. (I'm standing on the porch, wringing my hands.) That's not right, either, now is it? But that's the way things are. That's the goddamn way things are, and you better get used to it.

Malcolm turns to me, that gentle look in his eyes, that compassionate, hit-me-I-don't-mind, damned Christian turn-the-other-cheek look in his eyes. Oh, how I always despised that look. How vulnerable it made him. Stupid bastard didn't have an ounce of fight in him.

Yes, dear, he says meekly. Yes, dear.

I wake furious, trembling with rage. I don't know when I've been so angry.

At four, I wait behind the screen at the opened kitchen door until I hear the three boys next door come home from school.

Benny! Benny! they shout. Benny, where are you?!

I get up from the table and go over to the door. Open it.

Benny's over here, I say through the screen. Next door. At Kujo's. And then I shut the door. Firmly.

The meek shall inherit the earth. In a pig's eye they will. Do you hear me, God? They'll inherit the grave, the bugs, the worms. That's what they damn well will inherit, my Lord, and don't try to tell me different. You and Kujo, God, you're cut from the same cloth. Who really inherits the earth is the rest of us. The rest of us stuck here with nothing but memories of the meek. The trusting. The passive and trod-upon like Benny and my Malcolm, that's what. Soft as his lamb's wool sweater he was. As baby blue innocent, as well. You're too *nice,* I told him again and again. You're too damn *nice* for this world. You'll never survive.

Well, I was right, wasn't I?

Small comfort.

pier

My sister and I clamber out of the yellow Karman Ghia and run, out of our mother's sight, without looking back, run way, way down to the end of the pier where you must either turn back, jump onto a crab boat, or descend to your swimming lesson. Every day for two months each year we ran – away, far, out – and descended, leapt into the sea. She – our mother – was gone for the day; our life was ours. No weeding of pansy beds here in the salty wind. No pushing wheelbarrows of horse manure on this wet, grey beach. No sweeping steps by these chunk piles of granite. No Useless girls, no Heartless, Selfish, Thoughtless girls.

Neither of us with salt in our eyes or hair now, neither of our mouths gasping to swallow, neither of us fearing to drown. There is no stubbing our toes as we flee our mother. Can you remember us then, Kate? A third our present age? Running the straight, long length of the pier, warm wood under our bare feet, the warm beads of spike heads under our toes.

Kate? I say to your answering machine. I wish you were home. I want to tell you I'm pregnant! I'm serious! Call me? Please?

The trestle that crosses the river near my house is like White Rock's pier, but goes across, joins sides, doesn't jut out into endless sea, or make you turn back at a breakwater. But still it makes me think of our summers, of you. If we ran together along this wooden structure, we would run *with* the grain of wood. We would run perpendicular to the water's range of flow, and we could not run side by side – one of us would *have* to be behind the other.

Tides, planks, sand,
 Wind, salt, cries.
 Along the breakwater, gulls and pigeons cluster.
 Geronimo!
 Boys jump off the pier on the beach side of the crab boat moorage, swan dives or cannon balls. They bob back to the surface and flick long, wet lashes of hair from their eyes, and a strong, unschooled crawl takes them back to the pier. Don't need no fucking lessons.
 Geronimo!

Boys. Those are bad boys, aren't they Kate?

Shut *up*, Jessie.

Aren't they, though?

How would I know? Hurry up. We're late.

Of course, this trestle bridge carries its railway tracks alongside, while at White Rock, to reach pier or beach you must cross the tracks on crushed granite, tracks on a T to the pier. And here you cannot descend concrete steps and go underneath into dark, make-shiver cold and wetness, where crabs and mussels cling to thick, black, oily posts.

Bad things happen underneath, Jess, you whisper to me ominously after our lessons, as we start slowly back down the pier. Bad things happen below.

Below where? I say. As we walk we can hear the boys underneath, robbing the nests of the gulls. Later on the beach we will see the boys walk cockily by, the baby gulls cradled in their jackets.

You know. The belt.

No I don't. Belt? I don't get it.

You know.

Kate, *I don't.*

You're so dense, Jess. Shut *up*.

We are heading for fish and chips. Wrapped up in our beach towels after our lesson, pale, skinny, twelve-year-old me shivers with cold in spite of the sun, while you are a warm, brown, voluptuous thirteen.

A girl sits at the beach end of the pier, legs splayed, menstrual blood staining her white bikini. Whisper:

Kate, *look!*

Yuck.

Do you think she knows?

Of course she knows. She's showing off.

Showing off what?

You turn doubtful here, and your words come out slow.

How she's a woman, I guess. I don't know. Come on. I'm starving.

You shake so much vinegar onto your fish and chips that they are awash, and the smell gags you on each bite. This is how you like them.

Katharine, our mother said one morning as she dropped us off, Keep Your Sister Out Of The Sun. See She Doesn't Burn.

You are somehow my protector, then, I pondered, as we ran (late, always late). Why do I need protecting and you don't? What sets us apart? Is it breasts?

Some days when I walk across the trestle I can feel myself transported, flown. Can forget I'm in Saskatoon, can believe the boards I run along are to our lessons, warm under bare feet, toes tender for slivers and stubbing. I can see the gasping bullheads lined up on the warm wood of the pier, hunks cut out of them for crab traps. Pinned flailing to the pier with a jackknife. Bullheads. Just fuckin' bullheads, say those boys. Who fuckin' cares?

124

Here, Canada geese, cormorants, huge white pelicans rest and squawk and feed from sandy islands that appear and disappear one day to the next like memories; and like memories, the same ones tend to come back, but according to a dam man's whim, not the planet's revolutions. Gulls the most common denominator. And the sand.

I am not a prairie girl. I ache for the sea, for moisture on all sides, and what I receive is sky and more sky, dry, blue, consistent sky, pressed seamlessly to the endless undulation of grain-coloured hills.

Follow the stick, make dashes, curlicues; step around hearts made by and for others. Walk to the White Rock and back treading only on wood – jump, from log to log, mince across twigs, lay down a carried stick when you're desperate. Shifting, wet pebbles under your feet, bits of dead crabs, broken shells; lacy mustard seaweed, slippery green sheets, and bullwhips, yellow and long, slimy tresses, bulbs broken and odiferous.

Towel and driftwood caves on the beach. Boys kick sand as they chase each other and a woman angrily sits up, topless, and yells, Fuck Off you little buggers, and, shocked and impressed, we see her breasts – both of her bare-naked breasts.

At home in my bedroom I have peered at what our mother calls my "spots"; they are just that. I have not seen your breasts; I only know they are there, and growing, and with them the distance between us. I long for breasts; long to renarrow the distance between us. Me in my navy blue tank suit; you in your turquoise bikini.

In the distance the Peace Arch, portal to the States, the line, across the line, America, US, down South. In the distance where Dad's boat is moored. Beyond the white, white marble.

Kate? I say to your answering machine. I wish you were home – I called last week and couldn't get you. Did you get my message? I'm pregnant! Call me, okay? Please?

What is absent from my life is salt in the air.

What is absent is the pull of tides.

What is absent is my sister, wherever I am; it is not just here in Saskatchewan.

You have removed yourself from my life, consciously, deliberately.

At the end of the afternoon we wait. She is late, late, late, again, still, eternally, our mother, late, her first, middle, and surname. Late. We sit, and stand, and wander, up and down, in front of the granite post office, because You Girls Had Better Be There When I Come All That Way To Pick You Up. Up and down, up and down, days in the rain, huddled in the alcove like match girls waiting for our tardy, terse, and always late bitch of a mother.

You won't call me.

There is no lull between lunar-guided waves, no soothe of whoosh, pause, whoosh. The weir's water constantly rushes.

My longing for you is not a constant like this, though a steady current lies below. Its tides tug at the lunar phases of my heart.

Hot chocolate at McBride's, where birds dip towards glasses of water on the shelf, endlessly, rhythmically dipping to drink. Red licorice shoestrings from the old people at the English candy store. Our father saved the husband's life, and they always remind us. We walk along the tracks, the oily smell of preserved ties hanging stronger the hotter the sun.

It's the smell that smacks the places together. The smell that started this sorrow's coursing. Oil on railway ties in the hot sun. Trestle bridge, pier. White Rock, Saskatoon. The smell transcends place. Tracks and beds. Travelling north to south, bank to bank.

Kate? I miscarried.

Vinegar.
    Coppertone.
    Hot chocolate.
    The sea – salt and sand.

the almost *dead*

*t*he night before I left, my husband's buddy Ted came over after supper to help him pack the cube van I'd rented. They loaded the whole darn thing so expertly it was like they'd spent weeks planning it. Didn't take them more than an hour. When they were finished, Marty got a couple of beers out of the fridge, and turned on the game. Invited Ted – but not me – to join him. Then he got his Tupperware container out from under the *TV Guide* and rolled a couple of joints, and the two old high school buddies lay back on each end of the reclining La-Z-Boy couch and surveyed the TV landscape. I could have been gone for days already for all the mind they paid me. I sat in the bedroom, waiting. Waiting for Ted to go home so my husband and I could *talk*. I was leaving the next day. For Winnipeg. For good. This talk would be our final heart to heart. I would be as nice as I possibly could, after all that had gone down. I would be gentle: he was in pain. I would let him have his say, and then I would have my say. I promised myself silently in the mirror that I was going to do this straight, too, so that at least my leave-taking would be clear and clean. That meant no tokes, no beer. Not even one. This was too important an occasion.

I waited. And waited. I took a couple of star-shaped bath oil beads from my toiletry bag and had a long bath. I shaved my legs. Resisted putting on Marty's favourite perfume – it wouldn't be fair. I rechecked my suitcase for the purple sweater I couldn't remember packing. I went over my checklist a few more times. Have lunch with Rebecca. Check. Divvy up money from savings account. Check. Then I went through Marty's drawers to see if there was anything in them I ought to have, but there was just one old T-shirt I bought him years ago and really liked on me. I stuffed it into the suitcase. Then I thought, to do things right I should repack the bag one more time.

It got to be bedtime – ten-thirty – Marty knows that – and past bedtime, and still Ted sat there beside Marty on the couch, both of them half-cut and high. I have never liked Ted. He isn't good for Marty, and I've told him so. I don't hesitate to come out and say what I mean. Not like some people. Saying one thing and acting another. Nobody's ever going to call *me* a hypocrite.

"'Nother brew?" I hear my husband ask in his middle-of-a-toke voice.

"No, no," I whisper, watching them through the crack in the bedroom door. "Go home, Ted! Go home!"

"Sure, bud," Ted replies, putting down his cigarette to reach for the lighter. The joint has gone out in the ashtray.

I slam the door. Kick it, and instantly regret my action. There's no keyhole on this kind of door. Now I can't see what they're doing. Which, granted, isn't a whole hell of a lot, but. You asshole, Ted, I say to myself.

Patience isn't my strong suit, and before long I start to fume. I don't get it, I mutter, pacing back and forth between window and mirror. Why doesn't Marty ask him to leave? I stop. Maybe I do get it. Maybe this is it: as long as those guys sit there together, I can't say goodbye, and since I can't leave without saying goodbye, then as long as Ted stays I can't go. Maybe in his heart Marty doesn't want me to go. Poor guy. Now, Marty couldn't plan something like that consciously, I know, but unconsciously? Maybe that's what's going on. Who's to say? Or how about this. The longer the goodbyes are postponed, the longer the pain of facing the truth, the reality of my permanent departure, is postponed. That sounds pretty good too.

Maybe, maybe, maybe. Oh, who knows, I say to myself. Maybe it's just that it's Monday night and this is what you guys usually do on Monday night, which is part of why I'm leaving in the first place. This football, this hockey, this weird form of frigging meditation. When you get loaded you need something to focus your attention on, don't you, because you sure as hell don't indulge in hopes of a mystical experience like those Mexicans who eat peyote buttons. Nope. You're not trying to access inscape, are you, bucko? And in the meantime, I'm trapped in my own bedroom with sweet dick-all to do.

I give them ten minutes more on the digital clock radio. Eleven twenty-nine. This is getting ridiculous. I fish a pin and a small chunk of black hash out of my toiletry bag and I smoke that. Then, sitting on the bed, I have myself a little fantasy.

In my fantasy, it turns out that Ted and his wife are breaking up too. Turns out that a day or two after I go, Ted moves in with Marty so they can share costs and "batch" it.

I see the house as stagnant and still before long. Gloom hangs like Spanish moss. Mosquito larvae gestate in open rain barrels. The dust of sorrow and suspended time covers everything in the house. Even the door handles, because the men go out only to go to the liquor store and to buy rolling papers, and they tend to stock up. No one dusts. No one vacuums. No one cleans the toilet. They're a couple of complete deadbeats. But they're still breathing, so they must be the what? The Almost Dead. I like that.

Not that *I'm* exactly living, cooped up in here like this all by myself with sweet tweet to do. I take the miniature of Grand Marnier out of my purse. I was saving it for my morning coffee, but so much for that. I sip out of the little bottle and continue.

These men, these Almost Dead men, have lost their lives along with their marriages. There is a sense of relief in the casting off of responsibility. There is also pain, but that can be cured. "We have the technology," they say to each other in unison, and laugh a little, tapping their beer cans together in a toast. Night after night they sit together stunned, and stoned, in retreat at the TV.

Beers in hand and more in the fridge, and in flats beside the fridge, and always, always there are the figures of men moving, men moving, within the frame of that small screen, reassuring them that life goes on; men win, men lose, sure, sometimes, but always, always men *do.* *Things.* Even if what they're *doing* is sitting on the couch. The Almost Dead men watch and they watch and they watch that screen with a concentration and focus they never waste on their lives. And meanwhile, in their personal relationships, they do not really know what hit them or why, and by God they're not going to find out if they can help it.

Not bad, I think, finishing off the G.M. and screwing the little cap back on the bottle. I should write that down, I think. But then I remember why I'm killing time. I'm pissed off, remember? So I brush my teeth and stomp out to stand in the doorway to the living room.

"HEY!" I say, wiping my mouth. Their eyes flicker briefly in my direction. "This is the *Last Night.* I'd like to say *Goodbye* to my *Husband.* I'd like to say *Goodbye* to *You, Marty.* Alone. Please. If that's *Possible?*

They say nothing. It's like I'm not even here.

"Please?"

They continue to sit there like a couple of zombies, and then Ted takes a sip of beer and says real slow and soft and gentle, in the voice he uses to seduce women at the bar, "I'm not staying long."

"Thanks," I say, less loudly.

They sit there some more and some more as if they don't know I'm standing there waiting and waiting, and if this goes on much longer I might even cry.

Don't they care that I have to drive that big truck all by myself tomorrow, and it's going to be a long drive for a woman alone all the way to Manitoba? Seems not. The football or hockey goes on and on and on into eternal overtime.

I stamp and turn and stomp into the kitchen to see if there's anything I've forgotten, which isn't possible because I've been packing for weeks, trying to give Marty enough time to see that I'm really serious this time, and boy, he had better shape up if he wants to keep me around. He missed every opportunity I gave him, and now, here we are. Nowhere.

I get myself a beer, and I make a pledge: there's no way I'm going to let either one of them into the fridge again tonight. It's my fridge until tomorrow. If they want another beer, they'll *have* to do what I ask. In two seconds Ted will say he has to go home. So he can get another beer, is all. I'll say, Come back in the morning, Ted, and they're all yours. Marty is all yours too. But not tonight, old buddy. Tonight is *mine*.

Finally the game's over. The crowd cheers, and Marty pushes the mute button. Ted looks around as if he's trying to remember where he is and how he got here. He actually declines my husband's offer of beer number nine, so I don't have a chance to say no. He floats to his feet, and after a trip to the can he gives me a wave with his ski jacket sleeve. "Drive careful, Bonnie," he says. "Bye bye." Then he gives Marty a big hug. "Hey, man," he says, and heads out, pausing on the step to light a smoke. For once I couldn't care less that he's drunk and driving. Usually I comment, or threaten to tell the cops, which Marty hates. But tonight I don't. Tonight he can crash into a tree and kill himself, for all I care.

Marty is so loaded he goes "hee hee hee" after he closes the door on his buddy. Then he says, "Well," and he walks right past me. "Have a good drive," he says, and he heads for the stairs. He's been sleeping down in the rec room.

"*Wait!*" I say. "I can't go without telling you how I feel."

"Write me a letter," he says. "Mail it to me."

"But I want to know how you feel, too."

"You know how I feel?" he says. "Wiped. Bye bye."

"But Marty —"

He stands in the doorway, swaying back and forth. He looks at me with bloodshot eyes.

"You know what I'm looking forward to, Bonnie? I'm looking forward to not having ever again in my whole life to listen to you fucking analyze every fucking thing to death. *That's* what I'm looking forward to."

Then he starts down the stairs.

"Thanks a lot, Marty," I say. "That's a real nice way to leave things."

He stops on the stairs, but he doesn't turn. His voice is low, and hard, even if he is slurring as he speaks.

He says, "Who did you say is leaving things?"

It takes me a couple of seconds to think of a come-back, but I do.

"Well, it sure as hell isn't me," I say. And then I think how ridiculous that sounds, me with the truck loaded and suitcases packed and my coat all ready by the front door. But I say it again anyway. "Well, it sure as hell isn't me, Marty." But Marty doesn't turn around. He just keeps on going.

midnight at *the* oasis

*t*he bell tinkled above her head and the wooden screen door slapped behind her, catching firmly in its latch, as Willa entered Burton's General Store. The first thing she noticed was a small woman, crouched down in front of the old fashioned display case. The woman, a stranger, had cheap plastic sunglasses in each hand and on her head, and dust smeared on her face and on her green and navy Spandex suit. Willa glanced down at her, paused only briefly before resuming her mission. She was heading for the hardware section. Wire. Wire, and something else. What was it? But she hadn't gone more than three steps when the woman's voice stopped her in her tracks.

"Hello," the woman called. Willa's mouth forced itself into a tight, polite bow. "Hi," she said, and tried to continue.

"I'm buying a disguise," said the woman with a full,

wide smile. "Would you tell me what you think?"

Willa stopped. Her chest clenched and her breathing became rapid, as it always did with strangers. Why did she want *her* opinion? Anyway, she was *busy.* Her hands clasped each other and she made them let go and stay at her sides.

"What do you think?" said the woman. "Turquoise? Red? Tigerrrr?"

"I don't know," managed Willa.

"When in doubt, take them all," the woman said, still grinning, coming to her feet. "Right? They're only $3.99 anyway. Must have been born in that ancient old display case, don't you think?"

"Yes."

"How do you do?" The woman stepped out and offered a dusty hand. She wasn't as small as Willa had thought. About Willa's height, but more solid in body. Bigger breasts. "I'm Maidie. You live around here, don't you?" Reluctantly Willa took the proffered hand. How warm it was.

Though she tried not to, Willa ended up behind the woman in the checkout line. She focused her eyes on the back of Maidie's neck, following the moist tendrils, the glow of cooled sweat, to where the Spandex wetly met pale, pale skin and, here and there, the streaks of wetted dust. A compelling outward flow of warm, appealing energy emitted from the woman's body. She herself emitted a repellent, she knew. She could practically smell it; she could certainly feel it. *Eau de Go Away; Essence of Leave Me Alone.* It worked on nearly everyone.

As the woman left the store, she turned suddenly to Willa with another big smile. "Come for tea. I grow my own, and it's excellent. Chamomile, peppermint. Mine's the red house, south a mile. You must have seen my spectacular hedge. Stop by. I'd *love* to see you."

Willa nodded a vague and noncommittal acknowledgement and breathed deeply again once Maidie was gone. She was baffled; why was this person being so friendly, anyway? What did she want? How did she know she would love to see her? Maybe she was an axe murderer. Would she still be glad to see her? After paying Mr. Burton for the wire, Willa walked outside, got into her Subaru and drove the two miles home. She did not recall any hedge. En route she dismissed the invitation. It was easiest just to forget.

At the familiar turnoff, Willa entered the maze-like streets of her empty subdivision and followed the meandering black road to her house. Only one house, her house, had ever been built in what was originally intended to be an entire development. The landscape outside Willa's lot was brown and level, naked except for a few weeds poking up through the dirt. The pink plastic ribbons on the ageing and tilting survey stakes were the only source of colour beyond her beautiful lawn. As always, she stopped at the end of her driveway to look at her house. She liked to do this; it reassured her; she would be the first to admit that she was house proud. She had, after all, made most of the choices, and had done virtually all the decorating work and gardening. All Jared had supplied was the money. That was easy, since he had it, so in her mind his contribution to this house was in a sense much less significant than hers. It's easy to give what you have plenty of. But look at what she had created. She had every right to be proud. There was something of the *Country Homes* magazine about her place, as was her intent – the Casa Mesa design with the salmon-coloured stucco and orange-cream trim, the faux leaded windows that were always sparkling clean, the orange-cream planter boxes full of alternating gold and orange marigolds, the double oak door with etched glass paneling – these had all been her choices, and Jared went along with all of them. One thing in his favour was that he had always endorsed her creative spirit. She had pored for hours, days, weeks, over the magazines he brought her home from the convenience stores he owned. No one could say that this place couldn't be in a magazine, too. And her lawn – her lawn was as deep, lush, and perfect – as thick, luxurious, and creature-free – as a freshly-laid carpet in a Calgary mansion. Even the earth itself smelled clean. Not a weed in sight, and the lawn's edges look razor-sharp. There's a trick to keeping them that way. The driveway was so black you would think it freshly painted. The marigolds down either side (also alternating gold and orange to tie in with the planter boxes) had been this year's gardening brainwave.

But today when she stopped her car and looked out, the familiar and comforting stole of satisfaction and security did not descend to rest on her shoulders. No. Today when she saw her creation it did not reassure her. What was wrong? Neat and tidy but something not quite right, she thought. My place is like me today. Maybe it was just a phase in her transition, and would pass. She wiped a smudge off the rear-view mirror, some dust off the top of the steering column, and drove forward.

There was no one home but her, of course, and it had been that way for some time. Jared was gone. Gone into town, then out of town, for the day, the week, the rest of his life. He was gone before he was gone anyway, in front of the TV, teasing the dog, entering her in bed, reluctantly mowing the lawn. A layer of something around him like cool gas. Lazy, cool gas. Jared wasn't fussy about anything. He slapped together his life the way he slapped together a sandwich. Their life. She, however, was a planner, a careful, detail person. They spent a decade together, and some days, though not today, she wonders why she doesn't miss him more. She probably should. But how do you make yourself feel what you don't feel? Impossible. As impossible as denying what you *do* feel, she supposed, reversing the situation and then dismissing it. And so she had used Brasso on the clasps of his old fabric suitcase, mended the elbows on his sports jacket and tightened the buttons. Ironed his only tie. She had given him that tie for their wedding. She had felt like a mother sending her kid off to Sunday school camp, even though he was only going out to Cochrane, to open yet another store.

Willa drove up the driveway and remembered the instant her finger touched the button on the garage door opener that what she had forgotten to get at Burton's was batteries. Dash it all. That woman had made her forget. She slammed the car door. Bobette, the fat old dog, wagged her tail feebly and lifted her head an

inch off the pavement as Willa walked past her volumi-
nous form, then laid it down again. Willa opened the
front door wide and stepped in to another source of
pleasure: when she opened her front door now, she no
longer smelled Jared's cologne. Instead, she smelled
roses. Her homemade potpourri. She no longer saw
Jared's jacket and boots tossed off by the door. Nor
could she tell when he last had a beer or how many he
had had so far today from the number of cans or bottles
left about. She couldn't tell when he last shaved in the
bathroom, or slept in their bed. With Jared gone there
was no TV on, and nobody banging cupboard doors and
belching, no one telling her not-funny jokes, and no
one asking her where everything was when he had lived
in this house as long as she had. And, best of all, no one
pawing her. As she reviewed Jared's shortcomings, the
absences usually pleased her, but somehow today even
this was not enough. So she blamed it *all* on the woman
in the store. Why not?

Willa wiped off the kitchen counter with her hand,
then put the shopping bag down. She took the bottle of
Windex from under the sink, and some paper towels,
and removed the dog's nose marks from the glass door.
She put the leaf in the kitchen table and covered it with
old newspapers, taping them to the edges with masking
tape. Then she opened the utility drawer and got out
the hammer, the pliers, and the wire cutters, and lined
them up on the newspaper so they just barely touched
each other. Next, the white Lepage's glue. Then she put
on the kettle and got out a teapot and the tea strainer.
Teacup, spoon, sugar, milk in a little pitcher. While the

tea steeped she took the picture wire out of her canvas shopping bag and added it to the array of items. She went down to the basement and brought up her bird-houses, the ones still missing their roosts and roofs, and the ones that were ready to hang. She brought up the pegs and the tiny shingles. Set them out on the table. Plugged in the glue gun. Paused to listen to the silence. A pleasing sound. The buzzer went off at exactly five minutes. Milk, sugar, tea. She's ready to begin.

It has been almost three months. Three months of things staying where she leaves them, staying where she can find them again when she needs them. If it were Jared undertaking this project, for example, he'd have bits of moss on the floor, he'd drip glue on the table, and when he was finished he'd just walk away, never even really seeing the mess, and she'd be left to clean up. And that was life? No thank you. She was no servant. She was no maid. There were better things in life to do, she was discovering. She is free now: free, above all, to keep her house tidy. She has come very close to believing, lately, that the world can be reliable after all, that there is indeed a place for a love of order. She feels *validated*. Things *can* go the way you intend, pull no nasty surprises. There *is* predetermination, with a careful enough plan, and it is *okay*. This, she finds terrifically reassuring.

She rubbed her cold hands together to create friction, and when that wasn't enough she warmed them by placing them directly on the hot body of the teapot. That was better. Some people are warm, she thought, pouring the tea. Some are not. I'm just a cold one. A cold and bony one. It's *okay*. That woman in the store, Maidie, was a warm one. What a strange name. I'd hate to have that name.

The past three months has been a kind of transition time, she thinks as she picks up the glue gun. Like a period of mourning, and she is now ready to move on. To what, though? Well, she has given that some thought already. The prospect of facing all the rigmarole involved with dating even if she could find someone to date didn't exactly energize her, but she recognized its necessity, and her responsibility in initiating it. There are times now, she thought, as she squeezed glue onto the wooden dowel and pushed it into the perch hole, daubed off the extra glue with a piece of white cotton, when she would like more company. Times when she longed for conversations that took place outside her head. She didn't consider herself brilliant or anything, but she did, she suspected, have ideas sometimes which might be worth bringing out into the air. Sharing with someone.

She has never noticed the hedge before, or the driveway, and makes three passes before she finds the right way in. The rampant caragana hides the little red house well; the hedge is as high and thick as a castle wall. The kind of hedge a child would love to hide in. That Willa herself would like to hide in, except that she'd get tiny leaves and bugs in her hair. The hedge badly needs a trim, and something in Willa itches to rush home and get her clippers. But she resists. Maidie might have seen her drive in. Funny, the house hasn't seen paint in a dog's age and yet somehow does not look all that bad, and even seems more inviting than repelling. Truck tires full of petunias sit on either side of the screen door, which bangs gently in the light wind because the catch is broken. That needs fixing. Nevertheless, there is something comforting about this place, though Willa couldn't say exactly where that feeling comes from; it isn't logical. But then, feelings weren't, necessarily, were they? Maybe it's just that the place reminds her of *Little House on the Prairie.*

Maidie emerges from the house and walks towards Willa's car. She is delighted that Willa has shown up. She hadn't been sure Willa would, though she'd placed a bet with herself and taken it. Today she isn't in lycra or Spandex; today she is a hippie, wearing an embroidered peach-coloured halter top and Indian peasant skirt. Adapting to her environment, Willa thinks. Her feet are bare, and of course she is smiling. She is rounded, and the way her skin plumps out at her waist, and through the edges of the halter, is rather appealing in a fleshy sort of way. No one Willa has ever met smiles so much, or uses so much of her face to do so. As she gets out of her car in her apricot sweatsuit and pristine white leather runners, Willa feels in comparison that she ought to be going for a power walk, or making a trip to a craft store for more Phentex, not going for herbal tea. But this is how she is, she tells herself. And it's okay to feel how she is feeling. This is who I am, she says under her breath. And my feelings are valid.

"It's quite the hedge, isn't it?" Maidie says. "No one's

trimmed the hedge for a couple of years, and it's wild, but I kind of like that. No one can tell what's up here, and who knows what all makes its nest in there. I like that, too. Entrez." Maidie holds the door to her house open wide with her toe. "Don't give me credit for the tires," she says. "Know where I got them?" She grins over her shoulder. "I went out with a trucker for awhile, and they were a token of eternal affection." She laughs. "They're too goddamn heavy to move now. I did plant the petunias, however. That much I'll take credit for. They sell them at the store. Did you get some for your place?"

Willa stands at the back of a spindle-back chair and looks around. What a mess. The dishes aren't even done. And something smells funny, like incense. "Nice place," she says.

"Relax, woman," says Maidie. "Sit down and take a load off. This isn't supposed to be torture. I'm not going to attack you and chop you into little bits. This is supposed to be *fun.*"

"I'm a little edgy these days, I guess," says Willa. "I'm in transition."

"Ah. Transition," says Maidie. "You smoke?"

"No," says Willa. "Never have."

"I mean the good stuff."

Willa tenses. "A long time ago," she replies cautiously. "Once."

"Helps with transitions," Maidie says with a wink. "I've been in one for years." She points at a neatly rolled joint that sits beside a large red and white cut glass ashtray on the kitchen table. "For us," she says. She sits back down and starts painting the nails of her right hand. The polish drips thick vibrant fuchsia from the end of the tiny brush. Willa watches, tense, and tongue-tied. She is unsure what she's expected to do. Light the joint? What she isn't supposed to do is say no thank you, I'm too virtuous. But I *can* say no if I want to, she reassures herself. It's *okay* to say no. But then something in her loses patience and says, Oh shut up, you suck, this is pot, not heroin, so just shut right up for ten minutes and then we'll go home. In the meantime, be polite. It's not going to kill you. Weed. Pot. It's cool. Perfectly cool. Man.

"Fake nails," says Maidie, glancing up with a smile. "Shoot. Over the edge. How unlike me, eh? Hand me that box of Kleenex, would you? And put on some music?"

Maidie's smiles come so readily, thinks Willa, obeying. Maybe she is this happy. Imagine. Or maybe she's just high all the time. Willa can't choose a tape. She turns over the one that is in the machine. Maria Muldaur. *Midnight At The Oasis.* At least she's heard of that one.

"These nails are to scratch out the eyes of anyone who comes up my lane uninvited," Maidie says, laughing. "They ought to do the trick, eh? Just on my days off, though. Can't wear these babies at work. Would you call me Florinda for the day if I asked you to, Willa? Or Natasha? I'd like that. Hey, Willa. Why don't you grab a chair, woman? Sit down!"

Willa doesn't know what to say to that, so she just plunks herself down in the chair she has been clinging to and tries to look relaxed and casual. She looks through the open bathroom door directly across the room ahead of her, and she can see nurses' uniforms and stockings draped over the tub enclosure. On the floor, white Oxfords. A mountain of unsorted laundry keeps the bathroom door open and spreads into the bedroom.

"Are you a nurse?"

"Woman in white. That's me." Maidie strikes a wooden match on the side of the box, swings it around in a rapid, elaborate circle and lights the doobie. She tokes and then with nails like hot pink pincers offers the joint to Willa.

"You just missed the man from Colombia, Alberta, as a matter of fact," Maidie says through held breath. "He paid me a visit this morning. Here. Take it."

That was the smell she smelled. Willa takes the cigarette. Lifts it to her mouth. She inhales, chokes, coughs, inhales again. Maidie doesn't comment, thank goodness. Just takes back the joint when Willa holds it out.

"It's pretty good, isn't it? You ever want to make a purchase, just let me know," says Maidie. "I'll help you out."

"Thanks," says Willa hoarsely.

Willa stares around her completely dumb now and extremely glad she is sitting down. She can't even will herself into coherence or motion, let alone speech. I must have got off, she thinks. I must be high. It feels as though hours have gone by. My consciousness is expanding, she thinks. That's what's happening. Just let it happen. Be organic. Oh, if Jared could see her now. As Maidie works on her fingernails, then her toenails, Willa watches. Maidie's toes, Maidie's hands, Maidie's face, until Maidie's eyes lift and meet hers, and then Willa looks quickly away, embarrassed. Oh great. Now what will she think.

"I do love it here," Maidie says. "When I first got the shakes up inside, boy did they smell wonderful. They came straight from a mill in BC. I love the scent of tree flesh, don't you? Did you know that cedars are *orange* when you cut them open? I'm serious! I saw one once that had been hit by lightning. Bright orange, like an acorn squash. With that lovely cedar smell. There's nothing like it, is there? The wood in here's all dried out. But the smell comes back when it rains and the roof leaks. Or if I shower with the door open. I do that sometimes. I love the smell. Do you?" Willa nods.

Willa looks again at the pile of laundry and giggles at the change in it. Now it looks *friendly*. Not only that, she finds herself suddenly wishing for a gigantic heap at *her* house. At the bottom of *her* stairs. It would be so daring, somehow. Defiant. "Here lives a woman who resists order with every pore of her being." When *I* die, thinks Willa ruefully, the epitaph will read, "Here lies a woman who *imposed* order with every pore of her being." She looks over at Maidie. Maidie's eyes are closed, and she's swaying back and forth waving her hands like a demented conductor. She's pretty. *Send your camel to bed....* "Grooving to the music," thinks Willa.

She has no idea how much time has passed, but the scope of her yearning has expanded, and includes wishing that this whole house were hers, and that she herself was someone like Maidie instead of like, well, like herself, like some Year 2000 Doris Day. The expansion continues like a giant mouth slowly opening. She wishes more and more with each passing second that she had the kind of *life* that would lead to the living in such a place instead of the life she has led. How keenly she wishes that it had been *her* imagination that painted these wooden floors purple and dark green; that put cedar shakes on all the inside walls and made it look as though the house were turned inside out. It's so *clever*, so imaginative, and natural, and unique. Compared to her own house. What was not reassuring about seeing her place the other day, she now realizes in a flash like an epiphany, was that for the very first time, she felt there was something *unnatural* about the perfection. She had no idea why this unnaturalness should suddenly matter to her, because she has never been partial to either the natural or the organic; she generally finds them difficult to clean. But now her house, with its eggshell and sponge-painted walls and cream carpet, its cute little dried flower wreaths and cute little gingham kitchen curtains copied straight from a magazine, fills her with loathing. Its ultra-faux dining-room walls and pressboard furniture from the Brick. It all seems so *utterly* phony now. All that she had worked so hard to achieve. For what? So fake. And so she, too, is phony. She too is a fake. An empty, pointless fake. Before she can stop it an anguished animal groan surges from her mouth. Tears pour from her eyes. Horribly embarrassed, she claps her hands over her mouth, and her face, but still the tears come, and the sobs, and her hands are soaked with tears. But she can't stop, she is crying for everything in her whole life she has tried for, everything in her life she has tried to do right, get right, and failed at. She is a loser, she is *such* a loser.

"Willa! What is it?"

"I'm sorry. Nothing. I'm sorry. I didn't mean to do this."

"Willa what's wrong? Can you tell me what's wrong?"

"I have to go. Thank you for the tea." And she is out the door and at her car and inside. Locking all the doors. Rolling up her window. Maidie is outside, knocking on the glass. "Willa? Willa! Open up!" All Willa can think is that she has to get out of here, that her life depends on her getting out of here before she dies of humiliation. She tries to ignore Maidie's calls of concern, her knocking, she tries to find her keys and get the car started. At last the car is in drive, she is turned around and shooting back down the driveway, leaving Maidie in the dust.

When Maidie asked her what was wrong, how could she say something as stupid as that she wanted her house? That Maidie's house isn't what somebody else dreamed up and told her it should be, while Willa's house is somebody else's house, somebody else told her what to do and she did it. And what she had realized then was that her whole life has been like that. There is nothing original. Nothing uniquely hers. Nothing she has thought up all by herself. Nothing like the truck tires and the petunias. The shakes inside the house. How could she explain that she wanted them desperately because they were *real,* and nothing in her life any longer felt real. But that if they were at her house they would look *stupid.* And it wasn't anyone's fault. It wasn't Jared's fault, though she had blamed him often for everything. No one had made her do any of the things she had done. She chose what she chose. She chose stupid things. And now? Now she had no idea what she really wanted, or who she was. She wasn't even Jared's wife anymore, had no right to be wearing the wedding rings.

That night she works on her birdhouses, which are almost completed. Paint touch-ups, her signature, and the date are all that remain. There are ten birdhouses. One for every year she and Jared were together. They are all identical, miniatures of this house. But now the uniformity annoys her. These houses need distinctive features. Each needs to be as unique as Maidie's house. But how to begin? And what to do about Jared? Because when she got home from Maidie's she had done something completely foolish. She had left a ridiculous message on Jared's answering machine, begging him to come home, and now, with her wits about her once again, she is afraid he might show up. What if he comes? Heck. What a fool she is. What a complete and utter fool. Even Bobette prefers Jared, she won't keep her company; she sleeps outside on the front steps, waiting for him to come home.

Her bathwater is still running fast and hard when she hears the TV. At first she thinks she is imagining it, but the noise persists, grows louder. People cheering. A loud male announcer's voice. Soccer, or wrestling. Lying in the bubbles, Willa imagines how the sound and picture fill the living room, spill over into the hallways and kitchen, slide down and up the stairs and into the bathroom, the bedroom, the attic. Football sounds. Taking over her house.

"Willa? You in there?" Jared's voice.

"Mmm," she says.

"Hey Willa."

"Yes," she says, her heart sinking.

"What was the TV doing in the closet?"

"Not much," she murmurs.

"Huh?"

In the hot soapy water the rings slip off easily. She leaves them in the soap dish.

Jared fills the refrigerator with beer.

He fills her bed with his body. Covers her floor with his clothes.

"Come on, Willa. I've missed you, Willa."

"No you haven't."

"Sure I have. And you've missed me." He pesters her until she gives in. Afterwards he sighs.

"Nothing's changed, has it?"

"No. Nothing's changed."

Once he is asleep, Willa gets up out of bed. Picks up his jeans. Picks up his socks. Folds them and puts them on a chair. Wonders why his messiness drives her wild, while the mess at Maidie's does not. Is it because Maidie is a woman? Or is it just because she doesn't live here?

"You drive me nuts, you know that, Willa?" Jared is sitting up in bed in the dark. "Why do you always put *everything* away all the time? Jesus. They ought to put *you* away."

"I like things neat. That's all. There's nothing wrong with that. It's okay to be neat. *I'm* okay being neat."

Jared leaves right after breakfast. There is an air of finality they both recognize as Bobette heaves her fat old body up off the asphalt driveway and waddles over to stand beside his truck asking to be helped in. And then off the two of them go. Together.

Willa was nineteen years old when they married. Holy *cow* but I was young, Willa says out loud, taking the chamois to the wedding pictures in the spare room. Nineteen years old. Imagine believing all that. *That* stuff is all on the *outside.* What about the inside? Why doesn't how things look from the *inside* matter as much as how things look from the *outside?* Why don't the bride books talk about *that* ever? What are you supposed to do when your husband doesn't like to sleep with you? Whose fault is it? What can be done? She had tried so hard. All she had ever wanted was for it to be right.

Was it her fault that Jared's kisses had made her feel blank? She told him he didn't know what to do. She was mean to him, but she couldn't help it. She told him what he did wrong, she told him what he should have done and didn't. Knowing that what she said made him more and more uptight. But what else, she wailed, was she supposed to do? When she daubed the bedside towel between her legs after they had made love and he lay unhappily beside her she felt awful. Every time. Though they stopped, she still saw that look in his eyes for quite some time. His injured desire for her. She is glad for both of them that it is over.

The underwear and shoes from her wedding day she wore and wore out; they at least became part of her real life. But what do you do with the rest of the wedding things? she wonders, putting down the Pledge and the chamois and lifting down the Eaton's box that contains her wedding veil. Get buried in them? She spreads the veil across the spare-room bed. She takes her wedding dress from the closet, lifts off the dry cleaner's plastic and fingers the satin and tiny seed pearls. Plastic, covered with white paint. Pure fakery.

A trip to Disneyland would have cost as much as the rings did, and at least she would have known going in that it's all fantasy. In Disneyland you know the characters are wearing costumes, you know it's all make-believe, you know it's only meant to *seem* like a real spun sugar world that is momentarily in your sticky grasp, not the real one. And that the real one is still outside that gate, waiting for you. And Disneyland it isn't, no matter what anyone tries to tell you. Their wedding cost a mint, what with all those little paper doilies, match-books, serviettes, not to mention invitations, with her and Jared's names in mauve. All the fake flowers and lavender ribbons, the rented arch and punch bowl, the purple and white carnation centrepieces for each table. The dresses, the suits, the going-away outfits. Everything the book said to have, they had. We're doing things right, she told Jared, if we're doing it at all. It took them two years to pay it all off.

Who wrote that book? she wonders now. Who made

up all those rules about getting married, and convinced people like Jared and me that there is no other way? Look at that boy in his wine-coloured tux. Look at those black-trimmed frills and those shiny black boots. And look at me, beaming away like a little innocent under yards and yards of lace. Hoping with all my heart. For what? She used to be so proud of those pictures. And now? No.

Willa is outside working on her lawn when she sees, just beyond the sweet pea netting, a hot pink splotch approaching on the road. A trespasser. She frowns, even though she is lonely today. The person better not be coming here. People are supposed to call ahead. As the trespassing figure draws closer, Willa sees that it is Maidie, pink as a geranium in her lycra, pink as stick candy that has been in someone's mouth. She comes up Willa's driveway and stands panting, glossy, and wet, hands on her hips. Her plump breasts are squashed by the Spandex against her heaving rib cage. Willa puts down her scissors and covers them with her gardening gloves, brushes the grass from her pale blue sweatpants as she stands. That outfit suits Maidie, she thinks; makes her a firm and luscious piece of fruit. Their eyes are at exactly the same level when they stand facing each other.

"You home?" Maidie pants. "You home to uninvited guests?"

Willa can see the plum interior of Maidie's mouth as she puffs and blows from exertion. Her full lips are wet. "Okay," she says. What else could she say? "Sure."

Maidie walks across the lawn, over to the side of the

house where she unwinds Willa's hose. Willa looks at the footprints on her lawn. Maidie turns on the tap and sluices water into her mouth and across the back of her neck. "Ah," she says, throwing down the hose. "It's goddamn hot today."

"Your face matches your shirt," Willa says awkwardly, trying to be friendly. "You look like a big pink peach."

"Big is right," Maidie smiles ruefully, slapping her hips. "Alas. Sometimes I'm fighting five pounds, sometimes ten. Ten pounds of butter, lined up on your kitchen counter."

"I only meant you're bigger than a peach."

Maidie turns and looks up at her, surprised. "Exactamundo!" She pulls a T-shirt from her fanny pack and wipes the sweat from her face and neck.

"I made some lemonade this morning. Would you like some?"

"Sure. Your own private suburbia," says Maidie expansively, pushing the garden swing with her foot and making it sway. "What do you do all day?"

"I look after my house. I make birdhouses. Boy, if my husband could see me now."

"Why?"

"He thinks I'm a prude."

"I thought you broke up with your husband."

"Yes. He's gone."

"Shows to go you," says Maidie. "I bet you're not a prude. Must be weird being the only one living in this subdivision, eh? Like something out of a science fiction story. The only green turf in sight. Landing pad for aliens, doo-do-doo-do."

Willa laughs.

"So what do you do for money, anyway? If you don't mind my asking."

"Aliens bring me money," said Willa. "I'm in pretty good shape for the time being. Do you still like your sunglasses?"

"You know," says Maidie, "I confess that I always wanted to be enigmatic. The sunglasses and all. That's why I bought them. But enigmatic people don't talk as much as I do."

"I think you're enigmatic," Willa says. "The expression on your face is enigmatic. That's what I thought when I first saw you in the store."

"Really?" Maidie grins.

"Eccentric, too," says Willa, pushing the swing hard with her foot. *"And...exotic."*

Back and forth, forward and back, they swing and they swing, pushing the creaky structure out of its resting, pushing its creaky old bones into action.

"Do you like being a nurse?"

"Sure. But I'm a nurse only on the outside. Inside, I'm a ballet dancer. Jeté." She extends her leg, pointing it into the opposing knee and out again. "When I was a kid I wanted to be a ballerina so bad you wouldn't believe it."

"I don't know what I wanted. I thought I just wanted Jared."

"Men by themselves are never enough, silly woman. They just want you to think they are."

"Did you take ballet lessons?"

"Too bad for me, my parents didn't have enough

money for ballet lessons. Or time. After school we kids had to help Mum be the janitor at the school. Did I tell you this already?"

"No. Tell me."

"What's to say about cleaning toilets and mopping floors? Reeking of Pine Sol and doing your homework at your own school desk. Or the teacher's."

"*I* think you could have been a dancer. You move like a dancer. When you walk you kind of glide along, all graceful."

"Well, thank you, Willa. That's nice of you to say. I have worked at getting to know my physical self. I decided it was important. Most people are so dense about their own bodies, aren't they? Shove this in here and that comes out there. No idea what happens in between. No one taught us that, did they? Let alone how to *enjoy* our own bodies. I don't know about you, but back in high school I didn't learn a goddamn thing about my body, except from boys who tried to feel me up. Or down. Jamming their grubby fingers into me. Clueless little pricks, most of them. Grabbing my hands and putting them on their hard little dicks. And *in* school – remember health class? Remember vertebra and vertebrae? Now *that's* helpful information for your everyday life, isn't it? Tibia. Fibula. Duodenum sternum cerebral cortex. I still have the list memorized. That's all I knew. I liked the sound of the words. I liked to say them. But now I like to say words like vulva. Breast. Nipple."

"Don't," says Willa. "Stop it, please."

"Clitoris. Cream. Cunt."

"I mean it, Maidie."

"I didn't know how to make myself come until I was nineteen years old! Do you believe it?"

"No," says Willa, turning her head.

"Man," says Maidie. "Everything's so goddamn perfect around here! You'll have to be out there with tweezers if you want to find anything more you can do for that lawn. Makes me shiver to think of the chemicals it took."

"Jared liked it green."

"Do you vacuum your roof? I heard about a guy who vacuums his roof."

They laugh. "I'm not *that* bad," says Willa, wondering if she is.

From the subdivision road, Willa's house looks inhabited. Suncatchers glint in a window. The hose, unwound, lies on the left edge of the black asphalt driveway sunning itself in the waning autumn sun. The driveway and lawn are covered with leaves. The frost a week ago convinced them it was time to fall, but Willa hasn't been out there raking. She did bring up the box of toques, gloves, and scarves, brought up her winter coat and wondered as she did so why she is looking forward to winter this year. To plugging in the car? To shovelling snow? No. To the flannelette sheets on her bed. To the down comforter.

It is midnight, and the air is full of incense, and the ring of camel bells. Willa burrows deep into her bed, feels warm, feels hot. In bed, under the comforter, between the sheets, she imagines hands stroking her thighs. She feels fingers titillate her, duck inside her and out again, fluttering, trace lightly up to her breasts and down again. Once the orgasm subsides she finally admits to herself that she has felt the beginning of this arousal before. The almost audible buzz when their arms touched as they sat together on the garden swing and the golden hair on Maidie's warm brown forearm brushed against hers.

"When I'm with you, my hands want to leave my sides," she will tell her, though it will take a little more time. "I have to fight to keep them at my sides."

"Then don't," Maidie will say.

when it *rained*

*t*his trip, I walked into Dad's kitchen and I picked up the phone book. Eureka! There you were. This means something, I thought. Something must have changed. Maybe I am supposed to find you now. I always thought I might see you when I came to Beresford. Run into you somewhere, at the Credit Union, or in the liquor store parking lot, or driving your truck at ninety miles an hour down Leeman Road on your way to Pearson Roofing. But I have no idea what you're driving these days, so how could I recognize your car or truck? Maybe you're not even driving. Your record was so bad – maybe they finally stopped you! I've never seen a trace of you; I've never even seen your name in the phone book, though I've checked. It became an almost unconscious gesture, my walking into Dad's kitchen and picking up the phone book – done with the same amount of attention used to look in the fridge for a snack. I will say that wherever I am, in Beresford or *anywhere,* and I smell tar, I stop and revel in it. Instantly I remember the heat, and how hot the tar in a roofing kettle gets. Then I remember your body with your shirt off. Golden brown and sweaty. I see you standing at the edge of a roof having a smoke break. Leaning on a dripping, oozing, hot black broom. Foot on the flashing. Jeans and workboots shiny black with tar. How after a day at work your whole body smelled of tar and sweat. I loved it. Your body *and* the smell.

From time to time over the years I've wanted to get in touch with you, though maybe it was just yearning. I've done a lot of that. From mooning over Bread songs when I knew you, to Pachelbel, more recently. I have been subject to waves of nostalgia, especially when I'm high, or, in the past, when I was drinking. Whenever my present life wasn't going as I wished. Do you know the feeling? Aching to recapture something that never really was? Wanting another shot at getting it right, perhaps. "It" being my life.

What are you looking at, dear? asked Dad.

Oh, nothing. Just checking an address. I thought the bank might have moved.

Why would the bank move?

Well, you know Beresford. Not much is where it used to be.

That's true.

After lunch I took Dad for a drive. Of course I didn't tell him where we were going; Dad never had any use for you. Your wild driving and long hair. Your Fu

Manchu moustache. Your maniacal laugh. The one or two times you exchanged words you were polite, on your best behaviour, may even have called him sir. But no. You wouldn't have. People had to earn your respect. And he lost yours by not giving you a chance; once he had decided not to like you, there was no changing his mind, and he was barely civil. *And* you got tar on the upholstery of his mother's antique rocker. Black goo on pale green satin. That was the clincher. Remember that? You came over after work and I invited you to sit down and you did. And then there were the occasions you brought me home at four in the morning. I remember particularly well the time I went into the house half-snapped and half-dressed, assuming that Dad was in bed, and there he was, standing in the foyer in his pyjamas. The heat of your mouth still on my neck; the feel of your hands on my belly and other places. My shirt was open, my hair was a mess, I was doing up my pants. Dad looked me up and down in disgust. Oh hi, I said in a small voice. I think you had better go to bed, he said.

I love driving through my old haunts. I love rediscovering parts of Beresford which remain the way almost all of Beresford, except the centre of town itself, used to be. All green and uncomplicated. All cows and a few horses and acreages with mailboxes at the ends of the dirt or gravel driveways. The streets with names instead of numbers – Leeman, Carvolth, Berry, Johnson Townline, Glover. The roads named for families who lost their men in The War. Now the roads are known only by numbers.

When we got to what had to be your place, I said casually, Well, I think we'd better turn around here, and I pulled a car's length into your driveway, and paused.

They still have mailboxes out here! Dad exclaimed, delighted. Look! Remember our mailbox? Mailman needed a left-handed car to deliver mail. The whole box squeaked as it was turned sideways if there was mail. I never could get the oil to reach all the way in. The front hatch opened up and you reached inside.

I remember, Dad. I liked it when you sent me down to the end of our driveway to check the mail. I worshipped you, you know.

You did! I don't recall that. What's the name on that box there?

I don't know.

Pull a little closer. Maxwell. Is that what it says?

I think so.

Maxwell. How do I know that name?

There was a realtor named Maxwell. And I had a boyfriend named Darren Maxwell when I was eighteen.

That's right. One of your prizes, wasn't he?

I liked him.

Wasn't he the one who was in all those car accidents?

Yes.

Wasn't he the one who got tar on my mother's rocking chair?

Yes.

I remember *him*. One of your prizes, all right.

A gravel driveway straight in. An unlived-in-looking mobile home sitting in the field about fifteen yards off the road and to the left. Farther back, at the end of the driveway, a long, low, red brick house with dark brown wood trim. Three pickup trucks parked out front. Lots and lots of trees around. A very pretty piece of land.

A big dog started barking. I felt a buzz of nervousness: what if you were home? What if you walked out of your house? Saw the Saskatchewan plates at the end of your driveway? You might know it was me. I wasn't ready for that. Especially not with Dad here. I turned the car around, and Dad and I went home along 216th. The resurfaced roads are so wide and smooth, and there are speed limit signs. Life is duller here now. In the old days, Darren, you and I used to sail along these bumpy, pockmarked, unpredictable roads at a million miles an hour. Deep Purple's *Machinehead* blasting "Highway Star." A magnum of Andrés, a deck of smokes, and thou. How many Friday and Saturday nights? And if it was raining, there were weeknights as well, because rain meant you couldn't roof the next day.

The sum of my knowledge about what you've been doing in the twenty-plus years since I left Beresford is as follows: You moved in with a girl not long after I left – you met her when you picked her up hitchhiking. You didn't marry, but you lived with her and had a child, a son. Next, you were a Born-Again, a Found-The-Lord-Our-Saviour. Then you ran off with the babysitter. I smiled to myself when I heard this part: what would the Born-Agains make of that? My then-husband, Jim, and I talked about the Lake of Burning Fire, and how he and I were both headed there because we hadn't been saved. If it's as hot as they say it is, Jim said, we'll have to take a lot of beer.

You had the dubious distinction of having the worst driving record of anyone in BC. I don't know why ICBC continued to let you drive; you cracked up almost everything you drove. Your father's old red Chev truck. Your brown Barracuda. Your big red Chrysler convertible. That old blue station wagon. We fooled around in every one of them before you wrote them off.

But you never cracked up your brothers' cars, the beige Buick Wildcat with the 427, and the snazzy green Ford Torino, and you never cracked up your father's dark green Plymouth. You were careful with them. You were a fool, some said, a generous, sensitive fool. No one in our group of friends would lend you a car, even to go for smokes or beer. No one trusted you except me. And no one knew why you drove like a wild man.

You were never hurt in the accidents, though the cars and trucks were totalled. Surely there was some kind of caul that protected you – there had to be. And for me? I was never hurt either. Much. A broken nose when we rolled the red Chrysler at the top of Campbell River Road. Sometimes a bump, or a bruise. I wonder how many times I felt that sensation of flying through the air and waiting for the big *crunch* to come. The *thud* of reconnecting with the earth, and the bending of the car around us. The flight to the concrete.

Do you ever dream about flying? Maybe you haven't needed to. I did. I do. Feel the takeoff, the rise into the air, leaving it all behind.

Remember my '63 Volksy? Five bucks to fill up the tank. Forty-five cents for bulk oil. Up and down, back and forth, all through Beresford, Surrey, and White Rock. But mostly up and down past your house, to see if you were home.

Why did I do this? Because I had no life of my own.

I called Colleen and arranged to have coffee with her, and spent the morning loading up the back of my station wagon with junk from Dad's basement. Some of this stuff has to go, Dad, I said. You can't even move in here. Dad was quiet, and even helped a little. I guess I don't need this, he'd say, offering me a pickle jar. I loaded up the old *Popular Mechanics* magazines he used in the fifties to make the elephant slide, the playhouse, the surfing sailboard, the big round picnic table with the lazy susan centre. I threw in stacks of plastic margarine containers. Dozens of *The World of Medicine* magazines. Piles of old rags and clothes and plastic flowers and broken vases and a broken electric coffee pot. Cheesy spy and mystery paperbacks. I filled up the wagon completely.

And as I worked, I thought about Colleen. Going into this, I would have said that we couldn't truly be *friends* anymore, just *reminiscers,* if there is such a word.

I would have said that too much has changed between us. That our lives are so very different now, our interests too diverse. That when we got together, it could be only on the basis of nostalgia, and nostalgia always worked better when we were high. Or drunk. Or both. We'd re-enter our past and roar with laughter till our guts ached. About most things; there were things we wouldn't touch, of course. But now that we had both quit drinking I had come to believe that these trips backwards were kind of pointless. That friends are people who inhabit the present. I no longer needed to go backwards. What could be gained? As I've said, there were things I preferred not to recall. That broke, or cracked, my heart. Things Colleen had never apologized for. That always hung in the air between us. Or so I thought. Nevertheless, I called her.

Colleen's renting a house less than a mile from Dad's, up near the power lines where the gymkhanas used to be held. Up near Claynor Trailer Sales, which I see is closing down. Colleen's living with just one of her kids now, the youngest girl.

I pull into the driveway and Colleen comes out. She looks the same except that, as with me, being under a hundred and thirty pounds is no longer the most important thing on earth. Of course she looks the same: why wouldn't she? Her voice is the same, her curly, black, bushy hair is the same, her green eyes and her ready laugh are the same. You don't see our wrinkles or the grey in our hair until you get close up.

I've known Colleen longer than anyone except my own family. We were the only girls in our grade from

grades two to seven. In grade three, I arrived at Glen-
wood Elementary School each morning before she did,
because I came on the bus. I'd stand outside in the
teachers' parking lot and watch the Berry Road hill.
Colleen lived at the top, and before long she would
appear on her bike and zoom down it, and my day
could begin. She had a new autumn-coloured coat the
year I'm remembering, with fake fur on the hood. The
coat was brown and gold, like dead and dying leaves. In
Colleen's brown paper bag lunch were tomato sandwiches, and chocolate chip cookies, or nanaimo bars,
made by her mum, and she always shared or traded with
me. Sometimes she ate my Velveeta sandwich and my
apple. At lunchtime and recess we played horses. We
were going to start a riding school in England when we
grew up, when we were nineteen or twenty.

I worshipped Colleen. Admired her more than anyone in the entire world, sought her approval in *everything.* She was good at all the things that mattered. In
elementary school, she could play the piano, and she
could ride English. In high school she could flirt, and
enchant. There were *always* guys tailing Colleen.
While I sat in the background, green with envy,
painfully self-conscious, longing with all my heart to
be like her.

While I listened to Andy Kim, Colleen listened to
Uriah Heep. When I loved the Fruit Gum Company, she
was into David Bowie. I was *AM,* she was *FM,* in the
days when there was a difference. She was far fucking
out, she was Indian blouses and Greek scarves and Thai
stick and draft beer, she was the funniest person I ever

met and I loved her desperately, defended her fiercely.

I can see us at eighteen, when each of us had a VW (hers was a red '65), driving around in whichever bug had the most gas, with a couple of beer, and smoking skinny little joints of absolutely wicked pot. We'd drive around playing movie camera, the putt-putt of the VW engine the movie camera motor, the windshield the camera's eye. What a rush, man. Far fucking out. Man.

Guess where we're going before coffee? I say as I back out her driveway.

Uh oh, she says. Where?

To the dump. Now known as the "transfer station." To get rid of a bunch of stuff from my Dad's.

Sure, she says. I'm easy. How *is* your Dad?

The transfer station is out your way, Darren. Not far from the US border, between Beresford and Aldergrove. Colleen and I stand behind the car and huck stuff into the wide moving trough. Every once in awhile the bottom of the trough moves along, and all the things people want to get rid of are squashed and shoved through an opening at one end. Then they disappear. Gone forever.

In the old days, I say, throwing the coffee pot, we would have smoked a joint of Thai stick, and all this would be hilarious.

Well, it's pretty funny anyway, she says. But I'm glad we came here. I never knew where it was. I'm moving again at the end of the month. I'll need to know.

After I've paid and we're pulling out of the driveway, I say casually, Darren lives around here somewhere.

Darren? Maxwell?

Yes.

God, I haven't seen him in years.

Neither have I.

We drive along in silence for a while, and I get to thinking how this is landscape we have both been born in. It's as familiar as our skin. Our own particular countryside. Then Colleen says, I did talk to him on the phone not long ago.

Yeah? How did he sound?

Rita.

What?

I feel so weird bringing it up.

Go ahead, I say.

Okay. Here goes.

And then she tells me. Straight out.

Larry told me that you have always believed that I slept with Darren.

There is a pause. Then I say, *Larry?* How the hell would *Larry* know anything about it?

I don't know. But, Rita, I feel terrible.

Why?

Because all these years you have thought that.

Well, it's true, I say flatly. You did. You did sleep with Darren.

No, I didn't!

I say nothing.

Did I?

Yes. You and Rick and Darren and I went over to

173

Victoria. We drank beer and shot pool at the Red Lion. We went back to the motel. You and Darren went into one unit. Rick and I sat in the other one. You guys wouldn't answer the phone, or knocks on the door. We sat there half the night. Rick said we should do it, too, just to get even. I wouldn't. I couldn't. I slept in the bathtub.

I don't fucking remember *anything,* she says. She looks stricken. Why didn't you ever say anything?

What's to say? I figured if you were sorry, you'd apologize. You didn't.

Rita.

The times we saw each other after that were when you were still drinking, though I wasn't, and it seemed foolish to bring it up. I knew it probably meant nothing to you. You slept with all kinds of people. No one wanted me the way they all wanted you. I decided you wouldn't understand even if I told you.

Rita, honest to God, *I don't remember.* I don't remember *a goddamn thing.*

Now there's a great big silence.

That's okay, I say then, with a big sigh. It doesn't matter. Not like it used to.

But it matters to me. It's all *new* to me. I want to say I'm sorry, Rita, that I never knew. That's why I called Darren. To ask him if it happened. I needed to know.

What did he say?

He said it didn't matter. He said it just didn't matter and I shouldn't worry about it.

He said it didn't matter?

Jesus, Rita. With all my heart I'm telling you, that

whoever I was when I was doing that is not who I am. Sober I would never *ever* have done that to you. *Ever.*

Thanks.

More silence.

Oh man, she says sadly. There's a lot I did that I'll never know. I mean, what else is there that I don't remember? I didn't know anything about blackouts then. I didn't know *anything* then.

We drive along. Then I say, Darren lives right...here. Colleen? A part of me wants to go in.

Are you going to?

Yes. Just for a minute. He won't be there.

The big dog barks. Today there are two trucks parked in front of your house. We get out of the car. As if on cue the front door opens. A young guy emerges. He's barefoot, wearing jeans. No shirt. Smoking a cigarette. He looks like you at eighteen or nineteen, Darren. Just like you. It's eerie. Golden brown, lean and muscular, tall and well-proportioned. He moves like you, too.

Hi, I say. You've *got* to be Darren's son. You look just like him.

He grins your grin. He's clearly glad to hear it.

He's my dad all right. I'm Michael.

We're old friends of your dad's. I'm Rita. This is Colleen.

He smiles broadly; he must have heard of us. Wow, he says. Wow. Would it make my dad's day to see *you* guys.

Yeah? He's out? At work?

Nope. Down paying his taxes. He'll be right back. He'd be really glad to see you.

Is your Dad still roofing? I ask.

Not really.

What do you mean?

We were in an accident a couple of years ago. My dad and me.

A roofing accident? Or car?

Truck. We T-boned this guy. He pulled out in front of us.

Jesus. Were you okay? Was Darren okay?

We were in the hospital for a long time. He pauses. A *long* time. I don't know how long. We hurt our heads. Dad can't work anymore. He drives the truck sometimes, but he can't roof.

You were a roofer too?

Yup. But now I get these really bad headaches.

And your Dad?

He's changed. Quite a bit.

And then a truck pulls in. A man and a little boy of about seven get out. They walk toward us. The man, who has to be you, Darren, smiles as he approaches, says, Holy cow, what a sight. You two haven't changed a bit. The little boy lags shyly behind, hiding behind your legs. His father's legs? Must be.

What always marked you as you moved and talked was your energy. It wasn't nervous, pointless energy, but *life;* you had energy and enthusiasm to burn. Laughing, giddy, playful. You move with care now, walk steadily, carefully, toward us. Your chest and shoulders are broader. You're wearing a red T-shirt. Jeans. Workboots. A cap.

Beyond the wrinkles and the worn skin, it's you, all right. But in your eyes is this unfamiliar sadness. As though you have been irreparably injured, inside and out.

You got time for coffee? you say.

Sure. Don't we?

Sure.

There is a big electric organ just inside the front door. Giant stereo components fill up the anteroom. Boxes everywhere, some open, some taped shut. We walk around them and into the kitchen, sit down at a breakfast nook. You make coffee. Your son bums a cigarette from you. The little boy vanishes into another room and turns on cartoons.

From where I'm sitting in the breakfast nook, I can see into a room off the kitchen. It's full of creatures. I see three big tanks of goldfish. Five finches squabble and chirp in a cage too small for them all. A guinea pig sleeps in cedar shavings, a hamster sleeps in a toilet paper roll.

The coffee machine splutters.

So are you single-parenting these days? Colleen says. I know how hard *that* is.

I've raised all the kids. Mostly. Got this one when he was twelve, that one in there when he was fourteen months, and my daughter when she was five. She's away camping. They make my life a living hell. Just hell, don't you? he says.

Yup, says Michael, grinning. Keep trying to, anyways.

Oscar, the little boy, returns to the kitchen and stands beside me. He has gorgeous grey eyes. He asks me quietly if I want to see his frogs. We go outside together through sliding glass doors, onto the deck, and down the stairs. We walk over to the dugout. There is a young Canada goose in the water near the shore. It climbs out and the boy lifts it to his chest. The bird honks as he carries it around. You come out on the deck and call to your boy, You put that goose down, Oscar. He doesn't like that.

Yes he does, says Oscar.

No he doesn't. Put him down, Oscar.

We have goats, says the boy softly, putting the goose down as his father comes down the stairs.

Goats! I say. Aren't you lucky!

How did you get the Canada goose? I ask.

There was a whole family of them, you say from behind us. When the other ones left, this one fell into a forty-five gallon drum. I heard him splashing around in there and I pulled him out. He stayed.

And hamsters, and guinea pigs, and goldfish, and goats, too, Oscar tells me.

How many goats?

There were four you say. Two babies died. One got sick. The mother stepped on the other one. I had no idea they were so fragile. I guess goats are really fragile. There is a pause, and then you say, Like humans.

The invincible Darren, I think, and look out over the muddy body of water.

Coffee's past ready, you guys, Colleen calls from the deck.

Over the coffee, you say point-blank, My mother still tells me I should have hung onto you.

I laugh awkwardly. Feel eyes on me.

She'd love to see you.

I'd love to see her, too, I say. I always really liked your mum. I wish I had more time.

Do *you* think you should have hung onto me? I think, stirring. I'm the one you didn't want. I'm the one who whined and snivelled and showed up at your house in the middle of the night, begging to be let in. I am the one who hounded you. I am the one who sang every yearning, sappy song – every longing for love, every *my heart is breaking because you don't love me* song. I remember you saying to me, At *first* I thought you were The One. I really and truly did.

Your son was telling us that you were in a bad accident.

Yeah.

He said someone pulled out in front of you?

It was a guy who used to work for me. Him and his girlfriend. They were killed instantly. Both of them. They pulled out in front of me.

God.

You know what? They were naked. Both of them. They'd been at a party or something.

Jesus.

Yeah, it was pretty bad.

I move into your arms to say goodbye. Fit closely, naturally against your chest. I used to sleep with this man, I think. I used to have sex with him. This body used to be so familiar to me.

I was always so glad when it rained, I say without thinking. And I pull away.

Jesus, Colleen says when we're back on the road.

Jesus, I say.

Man. Did you see all the pills?

No. I didn't see any pills.

There must have been a million. I've never seen so many pills in my whole life. Jesus, Rita.

When I drop Colleen off, I reach over to hug her and I say, Darren was right, you know. It doesn't matter.

What doesn't?

About Victoria.

As I drive back to Dad's, I think, What difference *could* it make, now? That I was nuts about you once and you weren't as nuts about me. That you had sex, or didn't have sex, with my best friend. It launched me, in a sense. Forced me to depend on myself, not you, or anyone else.

I live far away now. I am in love with a man who loves me. I have grown scar tissue on a colourful assortment of wounds. I have wrestled most of my demons to the ground. I have my own boy, Alexander, who has my brown eyes. And I have the wide open spaces of a prairie that doesn't know traffic and photo radar. I haven't had a drink of Baby Duck in over twenty years, or a drink of anything at all for sixteen. Fast driving scares me.

Hi Dad, I say. I'm back.

Now where have you been, dear?

Well as a matter of fact, I've been visiting Darren Maxwell.

Darren Maxwell! Why do I know that name?

He was one of my boyfriends, a long time ago.

Was he that *roofer?*

Yes.

Now why on earth would you want to go and see *him?*

acknowledgements

Special thanks to Edna Alford, Carolynn Hoy, and Guy Vanderhaeghe; to the Canada Council for the Arts, and the Saskatchewan Arts Board; to David Carpenter, Joan Crate, Connie Gault, Scott Herzer, Daphne Marlatt, Patrice Melnick, Ellen Moore, and Roberta Rees.

Some of these stories have been published previously under different names or in earlier forms: "Nobody's Fool" by the Sterling Newspaper Awards; "You Are Not Yourself Right Now" in *The Fiddlehead;* "Quicksand," and "When It Rained" in *Grain;* "Walking On Air" in *Pottersfield Portfolio;* "Déjà Vu" was commissioned by the CBC for its *Festival of Fiction.* "Her Heart's Content" and "The Dog Next Door" were broadcast on the CBC. "Pier" appeared in the *Due West Anthology.* "The Almost Dead" appeared in *Sub-TERRAIN.*

about the *author*

J. Jill Robinson is the author of three previous collections of fiction. Her work has appeared in numerous anthologies and journals across Canada and has been broadcast both regionally and nationally by the CBC. Her first collection of stories was awarded the Howard O'Hagen prize, and her work has also won *Prism International's* fiction contest, *Event's* non-fiction contest, and a Western Magazine Award.

Robinson holds an M.A. in English literature from the University of Calgary, and an M.F.A. in creative writing from the University of Alaska in Fairbanks. She lives in Saskatoon with her husband, poet Steven Ross Smith, and their son Emmett. She teaches creative writing and English Literature at St. Peter's College.